Also by Hope Sheffield

Blood Mother
The Inflatable Man
Turnabout
The Glass Table

Hope Sheffield

The Poisonous Tree

This is a work of fiction. Names and characters are a product of the author's imagination, and any resemblance to actual persons, living or dead, is entirely coincidental.

To My Brothers
With Love

Chapter One

June 1998

"Let's get started. I think we're all here."

Perched on a loveseat in the Victorian style house her father had built for his second wife, Ellen Whitaker combed her manicure through her well-cut dark hair and ticked her patent pump to the click of the cuckoo clock. Ellen and her brother Alan had visited this house exactly eleven times before – every other year on Thanksgiving, and a bonus round two months ago on the occasion of their father's funeral. Despite the rationality which he exhibited throughout his legal career, Sanford Whitaker had lost his mind and abandoned his family two decades ago, when he met Cece Cavalier, a local actress twelve years his junior. Now Sanford was dead, and Cece and their teenage daughter Clara stood to gain a tidy bonanza, in addition to this appalling house, which had passed to Cece via tenancy by the entirety.

Ellen smoothed her skirt and checked her watch. She had depositions to read and motions to prepare, and she resented wasting time with her father's insipid second family. Her husband Mason Humphrey, a certified financial planner, smoothed a sprig of gray hair, straightened his tortoise-framed glasses, and nodded.

"Here's tea, while we're waiting. I'm sure Clara will be home from school shortly." Breezing into the conservatory, Cece set a porcelain teapot on the coffee table in front of Ellen, beside a half dozen dainty cups and saucers and a matching cream and sugar. For a woman who had recently lost her husband to violent death in the park next door, Cece looked composed, her gold hair freshly glossed, her peach shell and sweater set clinging tastefully to her middle-aged curves. "I'll be right back with the cookies which Jessica has so thoughtfully provided."

"Please, I'll get them." Alan's wife Jessica popped out of her pink chintz chair and beckoned Cece into it. As usual, she looked scattered, her mud brown hair a fuzzy halo, chalky toddler handprints stamped along the hem of her denim jumper. "I don't remember this teapot," she remarked to Cece. "Is it new?"

Ellen narrowed the ponds of her eyes into icy rivulets. If Jessica got Cece going on the subject of her collection, they would never get out of here. Teapots, most of them porcelain or ceramic, but some silver or pewter, lined specially made shelves winding around the downstairs rooms like a candy necklace. The worst were the animal themed ones shaped like teddy bears or splattered with lambs and kittens. Ellen didn't understand collections. It wasn't as if Cece had created anything -- Sanford handed her a credit card, and off she went. Undoubtedly he promoted her hobby to provide her an activity, to buy himself some peace. Well, since he had blown his brains out two months ago, he had peace in spades. He would never have to set his cup on another frilly saucer, not for all eternity.

2

"Oh, look, here she is. Are you hungry, Sweetheart? Did you have a good day?" Cece kissed her fingertips and waved to the Amazon straddling the doorway.

"Hello, Everyone." Clara Whitaker glided to rest on the pouf at her mother's feet. Cece stroked her daughter's sleek blonde hair and tucked in her bra strap. Clara was a pretty girl despite her tasteless jeans and the swizzle stick nose she had inherited from her mother. Really, it was astounding that either of them could breathe. "Last day of school," Clara observed, looking regally about her.

"And now you're a high school senior," said Cece. "I can hardly believe it. Your father would have been so proud." Sanford would indeed have been proud of Clara's accomplishment, despite his lack of interest in Ellen and Alan's high school graduations. He was too busy at work, he said, to listen to a list of a thousand spoiled children who had done exactly what was expected of them. Ellen might have accepted this if he hadn't also begged off every other event of significance in her life, except her wedding to Mason and her law school hooding – this, despite his fanatic attendance at all of Clara's badminton games.

Jessica emerged from the kitchen stacked with a bizarre assortment of mandelbrot, macarons, and smiley-face cookies. Judging by her waistline, she had been sampling such goodies for the last several months. A slight pudginess reflected her marshmallow-like character, perfect for her job as a preschool teacher at some local church or another. Jessica set the tray next to the tea things and sat down beside her husband Alan. Ellen didn't know why

Alan had married Jessica, but then, Ellen had married Mason, who, despite his Dartmouth degree and fraternity leadership position, was not exactly a human volcano.

Ellen gave Mason a look, and he cleared his throat. "Well, we are gathered here today – "

She snorted impatiently. "Just get on with it, already."

"I was pleased when Cece asked me to look into the family finances after the untimely death of my dear father-in-law, Sanford." Mason paused to look stricken.

"If you don't get to the point," said Ellen, "I may have to shoot myself too."

Clara turned white. "My father didn't shoot himself. He wouldn't. He loved me, he wouldn't do that to me."

"Of course," said Cece. "Your father loved you more than anything. It was a terrible accident."

"You have to say that, because of the life insurance," said Ellen.

"Shut up, Ellen," said Alan.

"What life insurance?" asked Clara.

"If everyone would please be quiet," said Mason, "I will explain everything." He extended his neck like a turtle and coughed. "Now, this is the situation. As you know, Sanford died without a will. Odd, some might say irresponsible, for a sixty-four year old lawyer, but who can explain the complexities of the human psyche." Mason pinched his lips disapprovingly.

"He didn't think he would die," said Cece.

"A strange attitude for a man with Parkinson's disease," noted Alan.

4

"Who killed himself," added Ellen.

Clara stood up. "Enough, everyone," said Cece. "The medicine was helping him. He barely had a tremor, and his depression had subsided. He seemed, frankly, frisky."

"Mother!" said Clara.

"For once I agree with you," said Ellen, glancing at Clara.

"Would you all excuse me for a moment?" asked Jessica.

"Shall I wait?" asked Mason.

"No, go ahead," said Alan.

"Anyway," said Mason, "according to our trusts and estates attorney, under the laws of intestacy in the state of Illinois, the widow," he stretched out his hand to indicate Cece, "inherits half of her husband's property. The other half is divided equally among Sanford's descendants, his three children." He nodded to Ellen, Alan, and Clara.

"That seems fair," said Jessica, returning to the room with a glass of water.

"Of course, the bulk of his estate does not pass through probate. All of his brokerage and bank accounts name a beneficiary on his death. Most of the money in those accounts, totaling about $8 million, goes to Cece. Each of his children will receive one hundred thousand dollars from a Northern Trust account. And the house passes automatically to Cece." Mason brushed off his vest and turned to resume his seat.

"You forgot about the life insurance, Mason." Ellen said.

5

"Oh, yes." Mason turned back to face the group. "Sanford left a sizable life insurance policy, $5 million to be exact, to Clara alone."

Alan turned bright red and made a fist, which he cupped in his right hand. Jessica stroked his arm. "Well, Clara still has her entire education to pay for," she said. "You two are both lawyers with a good start in life."

"Nice education," said Alan. "What if it weren't an accident – what if he killed himself? There goes graduate school at the Sorbonne."

"Well, that's interesting," said Mason, puffing out his chest. "There is a misconception that suicide nullifies a life insurance policy. In fact, the policy survives death at one's own hand," he paused to push up his glasses, "if the death occurs outside the exclusion limit, that is, two years or more after the date of the policy. In this case, Sanford purchased life insurance on his sixtieth birthday, that is, four years ago. So, whether the coroner ultimately decides that his death was suicide or an accident, Clara is entitled to the $5 million. Congratulations, Clara."

Clara turned pink and looked at the floor. "Thank you. But I would rather have my father."

"Sweet. But that doesn't appear to be an option," said Ellen. "What happens if he was murdered?"

"The same outcome," murmured Mason. "But I'm sure that's not the case."

"Unless Clara killed him," offered Alan. "According to Illinois's slayer statute, a murderer may not benefit from her crime."

Clara stood up again. "You are all horrible," she said, and she ran out of the room.

"Fleeing," said Ellen. "Not a good look."

"Nobody killed anybody, you know that," said Cece. "Sanford's fingerprints were on the gun. Which was his gun. Found right next to him."

"Convenient," said Alan.

Her nose lifted, Cece rose to pursue her daughter.

"Wait just a minute," said Ellen. "So, Mason, what property is in the estate?"

"Well, that would be the capital Sanford had in the law firm, and all of his personal property."

"Do you mean his clothes, shoes and ties, that sort of thing?" Ellen asked.

"Well, yes, but not just that. He owned half the marital property, half the contents of the house," said Mason.

"What do you mean?" said Cece. "I live here."

"Of course you do," said Jessica.

"You mean," offered Ellen, "things like the cars, the furniture, the silverware, jewelry -- teapots?"

"Why yes," said Mason, "unless they were clearly given as gifts. Of course, as I mentioned earlier, the widow owns half of what Sanford had to give."

"But we don't know which half," said Ellen.

"I'm sure we could find an independent appraiser to look through everything in the house and determine its value," said Alan. Ellen smiled at him.

"Mason, is this true?" Cece asked. "Some stranger is going to paw through all my things and give half of them away?"

"To your kids, Mom," said Ellen.

"I'm not your mother," said Cece.

"I'm sure you could offer to pay the children half their value," said Mason reasonably.

"No one really wants this stuff," said Jessica.

"We'll see," said Ellen. "All right, I'm leaving. Lovely to see you all, despite the sad occasion. Let's do it again soon – I'll call you. Alan, we'll talk later. Congratulations," she said, nodding as Clara reentered the room. "Assuming you didn't shoot Daddy, of course. Enjoy your summer vacation. What is it this year – digging latrines in Peru? All right, I'm off. Some of us have to work."

Ellen left her husband gathering his binders and filing them in an accordion folder in alphabetical order. Alan and Jessica followed her to the door. "Are you two okay?" asked Jessica.

"We're fine," said Alan. "It's not like we didn't expect something like this, considering Dad's general attitude toward us."

"He loved you," said Jessica. "It's just money. And he didn't make a will – it's not like he cut you out of anything. And of course he would want Cece and Clara to be taken care of. You two are already independent."

"That's a very generous attitude. But I don't think he's given me or Ellen much thought in the past twenty years," said Alan.

"I've met friends of his who thought Clara was his only child," said Ellen. Her jaw tightened, and she flipped her hair. "Well, whatever, I'm out of here."

Ellen marched to her Lexus. She had a headache, and she didn't have the energy to drive downtown just to put in face time at the office. She would go home to Glencoe and work there. At age thirty-four and up for partner in her law firm this year, she was under a lot of pressure. If stealing her father weren't enough, Cece and Clara had stolen her day. If she didn't make partner, that would be their fault too.

Alan grabbed Jessica's elbow and steered her into their Beetle. He hadn't wanted to tell Ellen, but he was a little surprised at the money division. Sanford had been spending considerable time at Alan's house lately. After his Parkinson's diagnosis, Jessica had invited him for tacos to encourage him to reconnect with his only son. As a result, in the months before he died, Sanford had appeared at their Evanston bungalow numerous times. Alan would return from work to find his father in a "Kiss the Cook" apron stirring marinara sauce. Sanford's attitude seemed different since his illness. He had been such a work horse, but in those last few months, he was almost giddy and kept declaring that life was too short.

Alan walked around the car and slid into the driver's seat. "Sometimes I wish I'd been more generous to Dad. I know we gave him dinner a few times near the end, but it was hard to get over all the years he ignored me. He left when I was eleven."

"You were as kind as he deserved," said Jessica.

"Maybe if I'd been nicer, he wouldn't have shot himself in the head."

"That's one of the worst things about suicide, survivors blaming themselves. But it wasn't your fault."

Jessica started to cry. Alan leaned over the gearshift to hug her. She was such a softy. A lot of professional people, including Ellen, underestimated her, because she had attended community college and taught preschool at the local Montessori. But she was a loving and thoughtful person, and that mattered more than an Ivy League resume. He was lucky that she had married him. If all went well, they would start having children soon, and she would be a wonderful mother. And despite his lousy role model, with her direction, maybe he could be a good dad.

"Let's get you home," said Alan. "I'm so sorry. My family is terrible."

"They aren't terrible," said Jessica. Her brown eyes met his blue ones, and she started to laugh. As they drove south toward Evanston, the laugh accelerated into a nervous chortle, and then she couldn't stop. Finally she calmed herself. She reached over to pat his knee. "Anyway," she said, "I'm your family now."

Chapter Two

Stumbling through a tangle of fetal monitor cords, Dr. Alexander Bennett dodged his wife Shawna's airborne fist, which he had been nervously kneading as he attempted to magic himself elsewhere. He didn't belong here -- he barely remembered his labor and delivery rotation from medical school twenty years ago, when everything was diffcrent anyway. In the old days, women didn't have opinions about how to deliver their offspring. You came at them with an enema and a shaver, trussed them up in a bed close to the operating room, and stepped out for a snack. Sure, being the husband was different from being the doctor, but Alex's first wife Meredith hadn't made such a fuss when their daughters, Maggie and Lucy, were born over a decade ago. When he was married to Meredith, Alex had enjoyed Shawna's youthful lack of decorum. Now he wasn't so sure.

"Shawna, try to relax. You're wasting energy."

"You are a shit."

"The contraction is almost over." As Alex watched the needle head down the endless stream of paper spilling onto the floor, Shawna morphed from Medusa to mermaid washed up in a birthing room in Evanston Hospital. With her salty hair splayed and her eyes clenched in anticipatory agony, she looked like the previously owned version of the twenty-something receptionist-temptress he had bedded on his exam table six years before. By the time he had realized that her ardent protests that their love could never be may have constituted a calculated use of reverse psychology, Meredith had discovered his infidelity. Somehow he had hoped that he could have them both, the lanky young blonde and the sensible, faded mother of his children, at least for a little while. Given a longer lead time, say, a couple of years, his thrill at the touch of a manicured hand attached to a limber torso would have subsided. He would have realized that a ten-year marriage to a clever, companionable woman with whom he had made a family should not be trashed for the novelty of sex with a cheerleader. He knew that now. But, in her youthful enthusiasm for his adult expertise, Shawna had unfortunately scratched his back. She should have been more careful – Meredith was a lawyer, and a fair detective, as it turned out. And she wasn't big on sharing.

"Oh, look, the needle is going up again. It's going to be a big one," he remarked. "I don't know why you won't get an epidural."

All childbearing women were irrationally angry at their impregnators, but Shawna was really fuming. Upset that he had moved out of their house three months ago in hopes of reuniting with Meredith, cervical dilation provided a convenient excuse to lash out.

"An epidural is not part of my birth plan," she hissed, sinking her nails into his arm. He pulled away and stepped out into the hall.

Alex felt sorry for Shawna's suffering, but her wound was self-inflicted. Any sensible North Shore mother-to-be would request anesthesia and produce Baby over a cup of tea and a magazine. Instead, she chose to martyr herself, on the theory that squatting in a bush was better for the infant. Shawna knew as much about medicine as he did about yoga, which was where she obtained the information for her birth plan. She had initially proposed having the baby in a bath tub, but the hospital, thank god, had put the kibosh on that. Instead, they offered this birthing room, a labor and delivery suite tricked out to look like the Holiday Inn, but with I.V. tubing in the dresser and a forceps behind the TV. Well, judging by her moans, Shawna must now realize the futility of papering over the birth process with duckling borders and flowered bedspreads.

Poor Shawna. He did love her, in a way. He just hadn't realized the extent to which he loved Meredith, until after she had kicked him out and he had been married to Shawna for a while. Meredith did have a prissy side that he still didn't much like.

"Hello, Doctor."

A passing nurse in puppy-patterned scrubs smiled and nodded. She didn't know him, but he was wearing his attending physician coat out of an abundance of caution. Alex didn't plan to spend much time at that end of things, giving birth was a bloody business. As a gastroenterologist, he tended to work with older people – those routine colonoscopies practically printed money, and scraping off polyps had paid for the cottage-on-steroids in Kenilworth that Shawna was now enjoying without him, besides saving hundreds of lives, of course. Shawna really

13

should be more grateful – without him, she would still be filing charts and living in a run-down studio apartment in Skokie. Well, he wasn't going to let her ruin his day. He was hungry and tired, and he could use a cup of coffee and a packet of powdered doughnuts from the surgical lounge. First babies took forever. He wasn't going to miss the show.

As Alex reached for the elevator button, his pager began to vibrate. Drat, with all the fuss, he had forgotten that he was scheduled to round with a group of medical students this morning. Being a doctor created so many time issues, conflicts that his wives never understood and always resented. But what was he supposed to do, he had professional responsibilities, he couldn't drop everything because they were bored or lonely or had gone into labor unexpectedly. Shawna was in capable hands, and while, in theory, she might appreciate having a family member with her for support, she was so angry at him that his ministrations were doing more harm than good. She must have friends, and he would gladly call them and invite them to take over for him, if he knew their names. That's what she really needed – a close female friend, someone who had borne children before and could empathize and provide helpful tips. Alex pulled his phone out of his pocket and punched in the number he knew by heart.

"Alex, I won't do it. I can't believe you're asking me."

Setting her University of Chicago Law School Alumni mug on the kitchen counter, Meredith rested her head in her hand and closed her eyes. After Maggie caught the bus for her last day ever at Wilmette Junior High School, and Lucy, for her last day of fifth grade, Meredith had been savoring the twenty minutes she allotted herself to munch a bagel, sip black coffee, and flip through the *Chicago Tribune* before driving to the Skokie Courthouse to begin her day as a prosecutor. She anticipated a routine morning of shoplifters, speeders, and warrant evaders, followed by an afternoon at the mall buying cheesy tops and tiny shorts with her freshly liberated daughters. She also had to run the vacuum, change the sheets in the guest room, and lay in a supply of matzo ball soup mix and Wonder Bread. Her mother was coming to visit on Saturday, in just two days.

"I'm sorry, Meredith, but I have patients to see, and Shawna is struggling. If you could just give her some support, even for an hour, it would mean the world."

"I have work too, Alex, and I don't think Shawna would want me there. We aren't exactly buddies."

Although her youth, glamour, and inherent cluelessness had allowed Shawna to behave generously towards her at times, Meredith doubted that any woman would want her husband's ex-wife holding her hand while she writhed in agony in an unflattering hospital gown. This applied doubly in the current situation. Three months ago, Alex had announced that he was leaving Shawna in the hope of winning Meredith back. The fact that, despite their mutual love, Meredith wasn't sure she wanted Alex, probably wouldn't matter much to Shawna, who wasn't much at making fine distinctions even in her most lucid moments.

"Please, Meredith. Shawna doesn't know what's good for her right now. Think of her as some sad homeless person with her cup extended, begging for a few coins, a scrap of kindness. Yes, she'd be better off at the Salvation Army, but she isn't there, and you're passing by, with money for a cheeseburger."

"Okay, fine, but what about me? I'm not sure I want to watch her bearing your child. I mean, come on, Alex."

"I know you, you're bigger than that. Just think of her as a fellow woman, a member of the sisterhood who needs your compassion and experience. Please."

Meredith frowned. "I don't remember your beating the bushes for someone to hold my hand when I had Lucy."

Alex paused. "Maybe not. But take it as evidence that I have grown."

Meredith rolled her eyes and stared dejectedly at her breakfast. "Alright, look. Maybe I can make it work for an hour – but then you're going to have to come back. This is not my problem."

"You're a life saver. Thank you."

Alex hung up. Although Meredith was the lawyer in the family, Alex instinctively knew one of the most important rules of cross examination – when you have elicited the desired response, sit down. Still, he had a lot of nerve. Chugging a last gulp of coffee, Meredith slipped on her shoes, picked up her briefcase, and headed out the back door to the garage.

Shawna scowled in disbelief at the frizzy forty-five year old who had stolen her husband, and who now approached her bed of pain clad in an ugly pantsuit and an infuriating look of sympathy. "Where the hell is Alex? Oh, Jesus."

If anyone had told her how much this would hurt, she would never have tossed the birth control pills that she had promised Alex she was taking. People were such liars. They talked about the miracle of birth, blah blah how beautiful, and they completely skirted the torture, which was in fact the central experience. Sure, it hurts, they murmured, but if you concentrate on your breathing and think lovely thoughts -- what the hell was that from, *Mary Poppins*? Well, she was a goddamned physical specimen and an expert at making her mind a blank, but she felt like, when on TV there was a spiral down to a black dot before the next episode, she was the black dot, and all the swirls were stabs.

When she surfaced, the pantsuit was coming toward her with pillows, one in each hand. Normally, Shawna could take Meredith, who had flunked gym thirty years ago and obviously hadn't seen a barbell since. But now, with the cockroach on her back, Meredith had obviously decided to take her chance. Trophy wife expires in childbirth -- it would be the perfect crime. And it would almost be okay with her, if it would just make the pain stop, at least for a little while.

"Here, lean forward, I'm going to crank up the head of the bed and wedge these behind you. If you're sitting up more, your back will feel better and

17

the contractions will be more efficient. Oh, wait, just a second."

Meredith and Alex had obviously attended the same class on energy management and the expanding vagina. They made her sick. Shawna felt a firm hand on her shoulder and excruciating fumbling with her nether regions.

"Ten centimeters! Now you can push!" a stranger in scrubs announced brightly, as if he were handing her a margarita.

"I know it sounds hard," said Meredith, "but pushing will feel better. Hold onto the bed frame, and close your eyes."

The birthing room was the only place in the world, her bed an island in infinity, a moon in space. Voices were telling her to push, when and how, and she tried to cooperate. If she would do what they said, then the baby would come out, and this would be over. Weakly, she wished for Alex, but he wouldn't come. Instead, he had sent this witch woman, who stroked her arm and praised her and kept telling her to push. No one could do this for her, she had to do it, she had no choice.

"That's right," said one of the voices. "Don't stop, keep going!" And time bent, in the clenching forward and falling back, as she tried and tried to do the job, to be a good girl, to make the pain please stop.

"Okay, we can help you. Would you like us to help you?" Shawna opened her eyes. A giant Smurf leaned over her bent legs and stared in her face.

"Yes, please," she said. Finally, someone could help her. She didn't care anymore what they did, if they could only make the pain stop. And then it was worse, they were wrenching out her guts, and the witch doubled her over so that she was staring into her own lap. And it was like a science movie of a flower blooming, but this time it was a head, and then the rest of it, it was amazing, the miracle that the pain had stopped.

They were messing around at her other end, but she didn't care. She lay back and closed her eyes again and felt the absence of pressure, the peace, the warmth as blood soaked the blue and white pads beneath her. "It's a perfect baby boy, do you want to hold him?" asked someone, and she said no, she did not.

This time when she opened her eyes, Alex was standing there, and Meredith was with him. They were huddled together, holding her baby. It was like a witch's coven. Meredith was holding her baby.

"Look, Honey," Alex said. "You did it. He's beautiful. Are you ready to hold him now?"

"Yes, give him to me," Shawna said. Alex rested the tiny boy in her arms, and he put his mouth to her breast. Shawna looked up to glare at Meredith, who wanted to steal her family. But she had vanished.

Chapter Three

"Maybe a little tea and toast, Dear. I'm sorry to be such a bother."

"You're no bother, Mom. I wish you felt better. Maybe you should stick around for a week or two, so that you can recover and have some fun."

Meredith peered anxiously at her tiny, gray mother, slouched at her dining room table and looking distinctly unwell. Yesterday Sara had sounded perky, excited to fly to Chicago to visit her daughter and escape the Florida heat. But, as Sara noted after her friend Esther broke her hip tripping over an uneven carpet in the ice cream parlor at Independence Valley, at their age you never knew what the next step would bring.

"I don't want to be a nuisance. As my father always said, guests are like fish – after three days, they start to stink." Once a rebellious daughter, Sara tried to listen to her father's advice now that she was seventy-five and he was dead.

Although Meredith loved her mother dearly, Grandpa had a point. Comments about Maggie and Lucy's insufficient clothing (which invited the wrong kind of attention), and about Meredith's ten o'clock news ice cream habit (the worst time of day to consume extra calories), were predictable and easily ignored. But if Sara stayed a while, she was sure to root out the mess of Meredith's relationship with Alex, and that could hit a nerve.

She had, of course, familiarized her mother with the general situation. But when Sara posed unhelpful questions like, "Do you expect Alex to abandon his wife and baby?" and, "After he left you for another woman, can you ever trust him again?" Meredith turned off Sara's updates. Whatever she had to say about the quagmire that was Meredith's personal life, Sara would be right. And frankly, Meredith didn't need to hear it.

"Where are Maggie and Lucy? I've already come all the way from Florida this morning, and they're still asleep. I'm not going to be here that long." Meredith poured hot water into a mug with a teabag in it and handed it to Sara, who snatched the teabag out with the water barely tan. Dangling uncertainly, the teabag dripped on the quilted placemat. "Oh dear, this will stain."

"No problem." Meredith extended her mom-palm, repository of spat-out gum and apple cores, and also impervious to heat. She heard footsteps on the stairs.

"Grandma!" Although, at eleven years old, many of her peers had begun to roll their eyes and snort, Lucy maintained her childish buoyancy. She ran up to Sara and gave her a squeeze. "You feel hot, Grandma," she said, veering toward the refrigerator.

"Let me feel, Mom." Meredith rested one hand on Sara's forehead and the other on her sweatered shoulder. "You are warm. I'll just grab a thermometer."

21

"Oh, don't make a fuss. I'm fine. I just brought a little Florida with me, that's all." She spread a blob of raspberry jam on her toast and then left it on the plate.

Lucy poured milk on a bowl of Fruit Loops as Maggie dribbled downstairs. "Oh, Grandma, you're here," she remarked. As she stretched, her cut-off tee shirt sneaked higher to reveal an innie belly button and several inches of white midriff.

"Maggie, you're so grown up. Give me a kiss." Meredith marveled at her mother's restraint as Maggie's lacey underpants peeked out from the "leg" of her tiny shorts.

"Grandma, you feel hot," said Maggie.

"I'm just tired from the trip," said Sara. "I think I'll go upstairs to lie down."

"Shall I bring up your toast?" Meredith asked.

"No thanks, Dear. Just cover it with plastic wrap. I'll eat it later."

Meredith watched her mother lever up from the table and turn to leave the room. Every time she saw her these days, Sara looked smaller. Her shoulders tucked her face toward the floor, while her neck strained to keep her eyes forward. In her buttoned cardigan and neat navy slacks, she looked like a tin soldier that had been out in the sun too long. As Sara moved toward the stairs, she ran her hand along the table, and then the wall. Suddenly she stopped and began to cough, a deep, insistent bark. When Meredith rushed to her side and put an arm around her, she could feel heat radiating through her clothes.

"Okay, Mom, that's it. You need to see a doctor."

22

"I'm sorry. This cold has just been hanging on. I shouldn't have exposed you, it was selfish. But it's been six months. I wanted to see you all." Sara gasped and held the wall.

"I'm glad you came," said Meredith. "Maggie and Lucy, clean up after yourselves. I'm going to take Grandma to the emergency room."

"I have plans with Lisa," said Maggie. "Her mom's picking me up in, like, ten minutes."

"That's fine," said Meredith. "Lucy, do you want to stay home, or do you want to come with us to the hospital?"

"I'll stay home," said Lucy. "Dad said we might be able to see the baby later. We have a brother now, Grandma. Maybe you can see him too, when you come back. Hey, you're a great-grandma now!"

"No I'm not," Sara said weakly. She started to cough again. "Do we have to go to the hospital? They make such a big deal about everything."

"It's Saturday, nothing else is open," said Meredith. "Lucy, leave me a note if you go somewhere. Come on, Mom." Meredith grabbed her purse, slipped on her shoes, and gripped her mother's arm as they crept down the back stairs toward the garage.

"Certainly, we would be delighted to come." Cece glanced doubtfully at her daughter Clara, obliviously nibbling a granola bar. "Should we bring anything? Red or white? Yes, thank you, Ellen. We'll see you Monday at 6:00. Goodbye."

Cece set the phone back in its stand and turned to stare out the windows surrounding the breakfast room. The morning sun filtered through the young green leaves on the trees in the park next door, where two little girls had found her husband Sanford's body two months ago. Once, the breakfast room had been her favorite part of the house. She had loved sipping hot coffee and browsing the newspaper with the sun warm through the glass, and eating dinner with Clara and Sanford, the artificial light inside glowing, the dark outside wrapping them in a black cocoon. Now, when she sat here, she felt a tremble, a disturbance in the air emanating from the spot on the damp, mildewed bed where her husband had lain unnoticed, his blood sinking through crumpled leaves into the cold spring ground. His body was gone of course, but a few of his atoms were still there, in the park. Sometimes she could feel fingers pulling her, as if she also were a spirit and could move through glass. At other times, the fingers pointed accusingly, or the thumb stuck up and then pressed an imaginary trigger in silent menace. The darkness at night no longer felt safe. The world was full of terrors, and even houses with armed security systems couldn't keep them from penetrating their pores.

Cece moved to the cherry-paneled refrigerator and poured Clara a small glass of juice. Walking around the kitchen island, fitted with a grill top which she had never used, Cece admired the enormous vase of white roses that Alan and Jessica had sent yesterday after that awful family meeting. She couldn't believe some auditor was going to riffle through her things, pawing over her jewelry and silver and crystal. It's not like Ellen and Alan needed

24

money. They were both attorneys, just as their father had been. Ellen and Alan would say that they were simply following the law, but Cece knew different. It was spite, pure and simple. They had never liked her, although lord knew she tried. When they came for Thanksgiving, she served them pie and tried to chat, to ask them about school and their activities. But they were sullen and critical, judging her and finding her remiss. They weren't even polite.

What was her crime? Their father had preferred Cece to their mother – well, of course he had. April was a minimally educated, rapidly aging housewife who failed to make the most of her limited attractions. Some plain women learned to apply makeup, they exercised and ate properly and bought well-made clothes and had their hair seen to. But not April. When Sanford met Cece, April crammed her pudgy backside into ill-fitting synthetic slacks, her gray-streaked hair scraped into a cheap barrette in a style she hadn't changed since high school. She claimed that she was busy minding the children and volunteering at an animal shelter where she set out newspapers and bowls of canned food for flea-ridden cats and pathetic, yipping dogs.

Sanford knew that April just didn't care, that she didn't have enough respect for him to create the proper impression when they entered a room together, never mind the lack of appeal when they were alone in bed. At forty-three, he was a kid in a candy store, an attractive partner with a handsome salary, and with younger women, in high heels and proper clothes, laughing at his jokes and doing his bidding, at work and in the inevitable work/social gray area. But the children couldn't see that, they were too young to realize that sometimes being an adult means ripping off the Band-Aid. You would think that now, at ages thirty-four and thirty-two, and married lawyers themselves, Ellen and Alan would understand. But somehow they seemed still to bear a grudge.

Cece stationed the orange juice next to Clara, who set her half-wrapped granola bar on a flowered saucer and wiped her fingers on a cloth napkin.

"That was Ellen on the phone. She invited us over for dinner tomorrow night."

"I hope you don't think I'm coming. She hates me, and Mason is boring. Seriously, I have homework."

"You don't have homework. It's summer vacation. Besides," Cece picked up the juice, took a sip, thought better of it, and set it back on the counter. "They're your siblings, I suppose. You may not adore them, but they're your only quasi relatives, beside me, of course. I'm sure they're hurting, now that Daddy's gone. He was their father too, in a way."

"What do you mean, they?" Clara stood and straightened the collar of her polo shirt. "I hope you don't mean that Mason is my brother, because he's not."

"No, of course not. Alan and Jessica are coming too."

"What the hell is going on?" asked Clara, quite reasonably, Cece thought, despite the invective. "We never see these people, and suddenly we're all getting together for a family dinner? And yesterday they were way horrible. Way."

"Frankly, I don't understand it myself." Cece brushed imaginary crumbs from her silk blouse.

"They can be a little – difficult. Maybe they are trying to make amends."

"Or maybe they want something," said Clara.

"That is quite possible," said Cece calmly. "But if they do, don't you think it behooves us to find out what that is?"

Clara paused. "Do you think that they shot Dad?"

"Certainly not," said Cece. "It was a terrible accident. The police said so."

"The Kenilworth police," said Clara. "How many murders have they investigated, anyway – like one in their entire lives?"

"Well, maybe two," Cece admitted.

"And did they solve them?"

"I don't know, I don't think so. But they knew they were murders, I would imagine."

Clara looked at her mother. "I'm going to get my bag. We have to leave. Badminton camp starts in twenty minutes."

"Fine." Cece followed her daughter into the hall. "Well, why would your they kill your father, anyway? It's not as if he upset them, they hardly registered with him."

Clara picked up her racket and headed for the front door. "I don't know, Mom. But I'm not going to that dinner."

"I'm sorry, Clara, but I already accepted on your behalf. It would be rude to back out now. We'll go, and it will be fine."

Clara opened the front door, and Cece followed. It was a beautiful day. The snowball hydrangeas were blooming, and the pots of geraniums that Jose had set out yesterday next to the pillars on the front porch were a glorious deep red. She walked down the flagstone path to the Mercedes in the driveway and unlocked the doors. Clara looked charming, her elegant white legs extending from her flirty skirt, her rose gold ponytail bouncing behind her visor.

Cece herself had important errands today. She had a dreadful meeting this morning at Northern Trust. Sanford had handled all of their financial affairs, but now she would have to learn about stocks and taxes and so on. This was not an area of natural interest for her, but she had planned several fundraisers and was on a number of charitable boards. With Sanford gone, she had to man up, as they say, and she would. Despite the absence of a will, Sanford had left most of his money to her, and she and Clara could stay in the Kenilworth house and live comfortably without any real struggles. Cece had seen older women working at Macy's, women who had to work because their husbands had not been good providers like Sanford. Thank goodness that was not her situation. Although she missed Sanford terribly, of course, she and Clara had a lot to be grateful for.

"You don't think they'd poison us, do you?" asked Clara, as they drove by the park and turned left onto Kenilworth Avenue.

"We will be fine," said Cece, and she patted Clara's leg. "Now, tell me about your backhand."

Being old was terrible, Sara thought, closing her eyes. And only sometimes, late at night, did the awfulness have anything to do with the imminence of death. Worse was the constant stream of physical assaults, the bruises and creaking joints and sleeplessness. Every jolt of the car along the brick street sent a shock through her bones, barely cushioned with a thin pad of flesh. If it weren't for her seatbelt, she would now be a clicking puddle in the footwell of Meredith's Honda. But, despite her head's occasional thump against the passenger seat, Sara was almost enjoying this moment. Here she sat within inches of her beloved daughter, who was on a mission to protect her.

Sara had been alone for so long, and she was tired. But as comforting as it felt to be cared for, she did not want her daughter infantilizing her. She had seen it happen too many times. One small setback, and your own children, whose bottoms you had powdered, were pirating your car keys and emptying the liquor cabinet. Before long, you'd find yourself parked in front of "The Price Is Right" with some exotic caregiver who barely spoke English. And the downward spiral always started with a trip to the emergency room. Sara opened her eyes.

"Meredith, I'm feeling better. This will probably take hours, and then they'll be annoyed with us for wasting their time. Let's just go home." Agitated, she began to cough again.

"Oh, look, we're here," Meredith announced, swinging into a parking space. She turned to Sara. "Just do this for me," she said. "If I know it's just a cold, we can relax and enjoy the rest of the weekend."

"You worry too much." Even as a little girl, Meredith was a fretter. She spent hours on her Hebrew School homework, making sure she could recite perfectly if the teacher called on her. As a teenager, it was her weight, an extra five pounds that her mother couldn't see. If Sara dropped dead on her watch, Meredith would never forgive herself. "Alright, I'll do this, if it makes you happy."

"It does, Mom. Look, I'm thrilled."

Easing Sara out of the car and swiveling, Meredith's grin faded. Sara followed her daughter's gaze twenty feet down the sidewalk, where a willowy middle-aged doctor drooped over the wheelchair he was unaccountably pushing. As he came closer, Sara could see that the wheelchair contained a young blonde woman. Even without her glasses, stowed safely in her purse in case she actually needed to see something, Sara understood that the woman was beautiful, which explained the special medical assistance, and that she was cradling her baby, wrapped in the striped blanket that had somehow become the national symbol for a newborn. And as Meredith's hand tightened on Sara's frail forearm and the doctor greeted them both by name, Sara realized that he was her ungrateful son-in-law Alex, and that the woman, whom Sara had never met, but who, on closer examination, looked puffy and conniving, must be his current wife, Shawna. And this baby must be....

"Lex," Shawna said, loosening her grip only enough to allow them to glimpse his face. Babies were never cute in the first few months, and this specimen was particularly plain. "Alexander Bennett Junior, Lex for short. Isn't he amazing?"

"He's very nice," said Meredith lamely. With satisfaction, Sara noticed a spray of tiny pimples across his undistinguished nose.

30

"It's good to see you, Sara," said Alex. To his credit, he did not try calling her Mom, which he used to pull out occasionally, and more appropriately, when he was married to Meredith. And he looked, not exactly ashamed, but mildly remorseful. "What are you two doing here?"

"I hope you weren't coming to visit us," said Shawna.

"I remember visiting you and Alex in this very hospital when Lucy was born," said Sara. "You two were so happy, over the moon. And little Maggie was prancing around, so thrilled to be a big sister. Such a warm, loving family, I remember thinking." Sara, whose eyes standing up were at exactly the level of Shawna's seated, glared at her daughter's nemesis. Then her chest begin to crackle, and she turned to cough into her sleeve.

"Back up!" Shawna yelled.

"I'm sorry," Sara murmured, and she was. She certainly didn't want to make the baby sick, even if he were the homely result of an unfortunate coupling. She and Meredith turned their backs and crept toward the automatic doors to the emergency room.

"I'll be there in a minute!" Alex shouted.

"No you won't," said Shawna. "You promised to take us home and get us settled. And it's almost time for me to nurse our son."

Meredith and Sara slid through the E.R. doors, which fortunately closed too quickly for them to hear anything more.

Chapter Four

The nursery was perfect, the best that money could buy. Shawna had made sure of that, it was the goddamn least Alex could do for their baby. Lambs dangled above the crib, hand painted with vintage Peter Rabbit hopping through a lettuce patch. A dust ruffle skimmed the custom rug, cream with lemon shooting stars. In one corner, a coordinated Flopsy Mopsy changing table hid a load of diapers, creams, and wipes, along with the assortment of wash cloths, waterproof pads, and receiving blankets that Shawna's mother had sent instead of coming herself. "I'll only be in the way. You and Alex should cocoon. Send pictures!" Shawna didn't bothered to tell her that Alex had moved out. The situation was temporary. He was sorting his mental garbage, and then he would be back.

Alex had already spent the night last night, which was why Shawna didn't know where the baby was at the moment. Sore from stitches and the rough pad between her legs, she inched downstairs to check the bassinet. Gauze ballooned from a bow decorating its hood to protect Lex from what, dust? Yesterday morning, when he had dumped them at home, Alex had noted that, once upon a time, Meredith had

32

bought a crib from Sears for Maggie and Lucy. Well, Shawna hated to burst his bubble, but that was, like fourteen years ago. She didn't even think there were Sears stores anymore.

Smoothing her bathrobe, Shawna perched on the living room sofa to gaze at Lex, who was sleeping, but not in his fancy furniture. He ate almost constantly, every hour, and he hated being changed, he screeched an angry, gurgling soprano that upset her and woke him from a nursing doze. Then she had to rock him until his eyeballs rolled around and he finally slept. But as soon as she ladled him into the crib, he started to squirm, and then to scream, until frankly, she would have liked to put a pillow over him, just to muffle the sound, so that she could get some sleep herself. At two a.m she called Alex, and he drove over and pulled the car seat from her BMW and set it here, on the living room rug, under the fronds of a dying ficus tree. He swaddled and walked and jiggled Lex, while Shawna crept up to bed and blacked out. Alex must have propped him in the car seat and strapped him in. And there Lex slept, for six blessed hours, until long after Alex had ditched the guest room for work and abandoned her per usual.

She was achy and exhausted and shouldn't be alone, a new mother who had bled on the delivery room floor and didn't have an idea in hell of how to take care of an infant. She sat beside the baby and stared. He was tiny and helpless and he needed her. But as she stared, he grew bigger and bigger, until he couldn't fit through the door, and she knew he would never go away, that she would never be rid of him.

The doorbell rang, Westminster chimes that Alex liked, but which reminded Shawna of old TV movies where maids brought women in bed jackets their mail on breakfast trays. Glancing at Lex, she pulled her robe tight and shuffled to the door. Maybe Alex had sent her roses to make up for the disaster that was her life, or her mother had shipped a crate of oranges, which she would gladly fling at both of them. She opened the door and stepped back.

"Hello. I noticed that the baby is home. You should put out some balloons. This is for you." The woman next door, whose name Shawna couldn't remember, handed her a wicker basket bursting with blueberry muffins and English tea, and topped with a silver rattle. Semi-comatose and also stunned, because this was the woman whose husband was shot dead in the park two doors down, Shawna forgot to reach for the basket or even to say thank you.

Lex chose this moment to begin a purr that revved, like a time-lapse documentary, into a full grown yowl. "Oh, the dear! May I see it?" the woman asked, and Shawna stepped aside. She set the basket on the coffee table and pulled Lex into her arms. "I haven't held one of these in so long, not since Clara was a baby. Frankly, I'm not sure that I remember much -- you know, she's eighteen now. It seems to be dribbling. Do you have a burp cloth?" Her bracelets jangled as she gestured toward her St. John suit jacket. "I'm on my way to church, but I wanted to stop by. Boy or girl?"

"Boy," said Shawna. She took the basket into the kitchen and checked the card. "Best wishes on the birth of your baby," it read, and it was signed, "Cece and Clara Whitaker." Cece, she thought, it figures. She grabbed a dish towel from the counter and returned to the living room.

Cece had kicked off her pumps and was bouncing back and forth on the rug and making cooing noises. Her highlighted hair was pulled back in a gold clip, her lips outlined in a tasteful rose shade. Shawna handed her the towel, and Cece blotted Lex's chin. "I think he's hungry," she said. "He keeps snuggling into my blouse, to no avail." Cece seemed surprisingly comfortable with Lex's assault and handed him to Shawna. "Is your husband home?" she asked. "He must be over the moon. Sanford was so excited when Clara was born."

"No, he's at work. He's a doctor," Shawna explained, as she sat down with Lex and looked warily at Cece. She didn't know the etiquette for discussing a widow's shot husband or for taking off her shirt in front of her.

"Well, I have a few minutes. Why don't I make some tea. It's important to stay hydrated. And one of those nice muffins. They're from Patisserie Francaise." Cece launched herself toward the kitchen. "In Winnetka," she called.

Settling back on the couch, Shawna fiddled with her nursing bra and tried not to drop the squirrely blob off her lap and onto the floor. As she hoisted her elbow to prop Lex into position, Cece breezed in with a cream and sugar set that Shawna didn't recognize.

"I found these in the back of one of your cupboards, I hope you don't mind. They're lovely. A wedding gift? Oh, dear," said Cece, "that doesn't look very comfortable." She lifted Shawna's elbow and wedged a beige throw pillow under it. "That's better."

A tea kettle, also a surprise, began to whistle. Cece returned a few minutes later with a teapot, two mugs, and a muffin on a plate, which she settled on the end table. Shawna reached over and took a polite nibble, and then a large bite.

"Oh, I think I needed this," she said, dropping crumbs on the baby's head. She started to cry. "I'm sorry. This is embarrassing."

"Never mind, it's just hormones. Hormones and exhaustion. You should have seen me a couple of months ago, and I didn't even have hormones as an excuse." Cece reached for her shoes and slipped them back on her feet.

"Oh my gosh, I'm so sorry. About your husband," added Shawna. "You're so nice, and I never even came by."

"Well, you had just returned from your year away, and I'm sure you had other things on your mind," Cece said, gesturing toward Lex. "Where were you, anyway?"

"Orlando." Shawna finished her muffin. "Alex was doing research."

"These men and their jobs, it's always something. Sanford worked like crazy, but I always knew he loved me and Clara more than anything. And now he's gone."

"You're lucky," said Shawna. "I mean, that you knew he loved you so much. I mean, Alex loves us and all that, but ...." Her eyes blurred.

"Of course he does," said Cece. "A beautiful young woman like you. Once you're cleaned up and through this new baby period, he'll be more attentive. And with a new mouth to feed, it's natural for men to worry about providing for their families. It's a primitive instinct, they can't help themselves."

"Maybe," said Shawna, awkwardly shifting Lex to the other side. He seemed to be dozing, his lips puckering and relaxing. "I'm the second wife."

"Well of course you are," said Cece. "That's why you're so young and attractive. I was too."

Shawna looked blankly at Cece. She was old, even older than Meredith. She might even be fifty. "You were?"

"Sanford was twelve years older than I am, and completely smitten when he met me. He had a wife at the time, but he didn't love her anymore. We got married and had Clara, and we had a wonderful marriage for twenty years." Shawna looked down at Lex, sleeping in her arms. His mouth squinched into a lopsided smile, and his eyelids fluttered. "Let me pour you a fresh cup of tea, this is probably cold. Would you like another muffin?"

"No thank you, they're delicious, but I shouldn't. More tea would be nice. I don't want to spill it on him, though," she said, standing up.

"Oh, of course not, let me take him. What's his name?" she asked, easing him from Shawna's arms.

"It's Lex, Alexander, after his father," said Shawna. Cece nodded her approval as she jiggled the baby. Shawna drank the cold tea and poured herself a fresh cup. She looked at Cece seriously. "I'm afraid we're not like you. Alex has – an apartment. He thinks," Shawna started to sniff, "he thinks he might want to go back to his first wife. Meredith."

"Nonsense," said Cece. "They don't go back. Men get overwhelmed sometimes, and you've had a lot of changes lately, with the move, your pregnancy,

37

and now this adorable child. But he'll straighten out, don't you worry."

"He already has two children, two girls, they're not in diapers and up half the night, they're eleven and fourteen."

"Why, Ellen and Alan were about that age when Clara was born. Sanford's job was done, they were practically adults. And they lived with their mother, such a poisoning influence. Maybe he felt a little tug toward them early on, but once Clara came along, he knew which was his real family. I honestly don't think he gave the others a second thought, once Clara was three months old and smiling, and I had returned to fighting trim. It was such a blessing for everyone, a clean break. Sanford knew we needed his full attention. And Clara was so clever, so much like him in so many ways."

"Alex did come over last night."

"Of course he did," said Cece. "He won't be able to stay away. Mark my words, by the time this little one is three months old, your husband will be home with you where he belongs. Well, I really must run," she said. "What a beautiful cradle! Shall I put him in there?" she asked, lifting the gauze.

"I don't know," said Shawna. "I think he hates it. He slept in the car seat last night."

"Not very glamorous, but baby knows what he needs." Unfazed, Cece stooped to lower Lex into the seat. He wiggled, sighed, and collapsed. "His tummy may be bothering him, Clara was the same. It's difficult right now, but he'll get over it."

"You're so helpful, you made me feel so much better. Thank you."

"You will be fine," said Cece. "But I know, it's all new. I'll call you tomorrow, to see how you're doing. Maybe we can take the baby for a walk later in the week. Some fresh air would do you good."

Shawna smiled. She didn't need her mother. Cece would take her place. She would help out and teach Shawna what to do, to manage the baby and to get Alex back. Cece had done it, and she and her husband and their child had enjoyed a wonderful life together, right up until her husband shot himself in the head. Well, that was just a fluke. Alex didn't even own a gun.

As they reached the front door, Shawna heard a furtive knock. Cece opened it. "Hello, you must want Mrs. Bennett. I was just leaving."

In jeans and a faded blouse, her brown hair curling around her glasses, Meredith stood at the door, with Maggie, just visible behind her, looking put-out. "Meredith Bennett," she said, sticking out her hand, which Cece ignored.

"What a coincidence! Your home help has the same last name," she said to Shawna. "There are some tea things to clear away, and then I'm sure Mrs. Bennett will be able to tell you where to start, Meredith." Turning back to Shawna, Cece winked. "I'm off to church," she whispered. "You've got this." She swept past Meredith and Maggie and down the front walk.

"Who was that?" asked Meredith.

"That was my next door neighbor, Cece Whitaker. Not that it's any of your business. What do you want?"

"I tried to call you, but no one answered."

"Bummer," said Shawna. "So what?"

39

Standing in the doorway, Meredith studied Shawna. Her normally sleek blonde hair hung limp behind her ears. Without makeup, her skin showed the darkness under her eyes and a faint spray of lines at their corners. Her stomach protruded from under the bow where the sides of her robe didn't quite meet, and she smelled like sour milk and sweat. Even Maggie, who, at her adolescent worst, did not want to help with her new baby brother, seemed touched by the putrid version of her formerly hot stepmother.

"I was wondering if you would like Maggie's help for a couple of hours."

Shawna wrestled with her resentment of Meredith, her fondness for Maggie, and her urgent need to take a shower and eat scrambled eggs. "Do you want to come in for a while?" she asked Maggie. "You could meet your new brother."

"I don't know," said Maggie stiffly. "I have a lot of homework."

"I thought it was summer vacation."

"Whatever."

"Come on, Maggie," Shawna urged. "I miss you."

During the first three years of her marriage, Shawna had been helpful, watching Maggie and Lucy when Meredith had to work late. Granted, Meredith wouldn't have needed to work full-time if Shawna hadn't seduced her husband, but still. Then Shawna and Alex moved to Florida for a year, and by the time they came back, Shawna was pregnant. Maggie now viewed Shawna as a home wrecker who had magicked her father's brain from his skull and poofed it into his underpants. Despite some sympathy with this position, Meredith knew it to be an oversimplification.

Alex was a grown man with a will of his own. He had left his family and thrown in his lot with a young woman his junior in every way. And now they had a baby together.

"Where is the baby anyway?" Meredith asked. Shawna just glared. "Oh, I almost forgot." She reached into her purse. "I brought him a present."

Meredith produced a box wrapped in a print of ducklings and chicks and tied with curly ribbons. "He may not need this now, but I think you'll love it next winter." Focusing only on the baby as a baby, Meredith had bought a white hooded sweater with a zip up the back, the sort that Maggie and Lucy had lived in during cold Chicago winters. Meredith hadn't known quite what to say in the card, and had decided to address Lex. "Welcome to the world," she had written. "Love, Maggie and Lucy." She had no idea what to call herself in reference to this child and was determined to skip the whole thing, at least for now.

"Thank you," said Shawna, recoiling as if receiving a gift from Maleficent. With a push from her mother, Maggie slipped into the house.

"Call me when you want to come home," shouted Meredith. "Or, no, wait, I'll pick you up – in two hours?"

Shawna nodded and shut the door. As it closed, Meredith could hear the sound of a very new baby beginning to cry.

Chapter Five

Alex pulled Sara's chart from its plastic sleeve at the foot of her bed and tried to look important. Although chatting with the nurse just a moment ago, Sara now lay inert, her eyes pinched shut, like a child trying to disappear. Alex's relationship with Meredith's mother had never been close, and now it was circling the toilet bowl.

Observing her, a skeleton clad in a brown wool vest and skirt and breathing raspily, Alex recalled the Sara of sixteen years ago, when Meredith first introduced her. She was fifty-nine years old, pretty like her daughter, and sharp and energetic. Although he imagined himself a mother's dream, my future son-in-law the doctor, he knew that he was lucky. Meredith was attractive and sensible and smart. During his residency, she brought him tuna sandwiches and amused herself while he worked and slept. When he obsessed about spastic colons, she showed him the lake, its beauty and immensity. Sara fed them brisket and grilled him about his work habits, not to determine if he could support Meredith, who was, after all, a lawyer, but to assess the negative impact his ambition might have on her daughter's happiness.

Throughout their marriage, Alex had felt that Sara's jury was still out. If he had not received the guillotine after their divorce, he could only thank Maggie and Lucy and his involvement in their lives. Now he was once again trying to prove his love. He had moved out of the Kenilworth house and into a depressing apartment across from Plaza del Lago in the condo purgatory known as No Man's Land, exile for retirees, divorcees, and other deposed pariahs. This ought to placate Sara, but for some reason, her mouth squeezed and frowning, she still looked a little disgruntled.

"Sara, are you awake? It's Alex. I hear you're going home today." He could see her eyes rolling behind their lids. "I've come to discuss your discharge instructions." This was a lie, but he hoped that her desperation to escape might overcome her disgust with him. And he was right. Sara's brown eyes blinked open, and she shimmied herself up to a full sit against the propped bed.

"Thank you, but I have my own doctor. He just needs to sign a few papers. You needn't trouble, I'm sure you have things to do." She started to cough, but, thank god, a shallower croak than the wheeze he had heard outside the emergency room. He handed her a Styrofoam cup of tepid water and a bent straw, which she took.

"How are you feeling?" he asked.

"Much better. The nurses here are wonderful, so caring. I had Karen last night and Jasmine during the day. I don't suppose you know them."

"Not really," he admitted. "There are a lot of nurses here, and this isn't my floor. But I wanted to check on you, to see how you're doing. I'm happy to see you so improved. Is there anything I can do for you?"

"Well, first, you can tell me about your plans. With my daughter." Sara handed back the water.

"My plan is to get back together with Meredith. We still love each other, and we love our children."

"I see," said Sara. "And what happens to your current wife and new baby?"

"I will provide for them, of course," said Alex. "And I will be a father to Lex. It's my responsibility, even though this pregnancy was not something that I expected."

Sara turned white. "That's not my business," she said.

"Okay. What else can I do for you? Short of tying sheets together, attaching them to an I.V. pole, and chucking them out the window for your getaway."

"Exactly," she said. "Please find my doctor, so that I can leave through the front door. I've been waiting over an hour. And then you can drive me back to Meredith's. It's only four o'clock, and I don't want to bother her at work." Sara threw this down like a challenge. They met each other's eyes.

"Fine," he said. Exiting to page Sara's doctor, his mental rolodex of late afternoon appointments whirred through his brain. Well, his receptionist would just have to reschedule everyone. Emergency surgery, that was the card she typically played.

Ten minutes later, Alex returned to Sara's room. She was waiting in a wheelchair, a white

44

plastic bag perched on her lap. Her sneakers dangled above the footrests, and her flattened gray hair skimmed the top of the seatback. "This is Darnell," she said, indicating the orderly in scrubs hovering behind her. "He has two little girls, and he's studying to be a speech pathologist. He is ready to take me downstairs."

"Thank you," Alex said, nodding to Darnell. "I'll go pull my car around."

Gray coat flapping, Alex rushed to the parking garage to begin the endless swoops necessary to move his car from doctor's parking on the second level to the exit. He showed his badge to the attendant and drove around the block, to enter the driveway in front of Evanston Hospital. As he ducked and stepped out of his Mercedes, Darnell pushed Sara to the curb. Slumped in the chair, she looked shrunken and ovoid, like Humpty Dumpty just before his tumble. Fumbling in her bag, Sara's crooked hand emerged triumphant with a folded dollar bill.

"Here, Darnell, this is for you," she said.

"Thanks, Miss, I really can't take that."

Sara gave the money to Alex. "Here, just stick it in his pocket," she said.

Alex looked at Darnell and shrugged. "There's no sense arguing," he said and handed him the dollar.

While Darnell held the chair, Alex took Sara's bag and elbow and helped her into the passenger seat. He reached over her to help with the seatbelt. "I can do it," she said, swatting his hand.

Alex placed the bag in the trunk and resumed the driver's seat. Meredith's house was only ten minutes away, but this could be a long ride. "So, Sara," he began. "How are things in Florida?"

"Let's just listen to some music," she said.

Sara hobbled up the front path to her daughter's house. Alex drove too fast, and she didn't like him lurking next to her, ready to grab her, as if she were a toddler. She had been walking on her own for seventy-four years, and the flat concrete walk to Meredith's door was hardly a challenge, though a few of the squares did have cracks and bulges and could stand to be replaced. Glancing askance at the weedy beds of withered tulips that lined the east side of the property, Sara considered her daughter's choices. If Meredith had looked about her earlier, at University of Chicago Law School, surely she could have found a more devoted, handier husband than Alex, who was good for little besides wiring money into their checking account and then dumping her when a dumb blonde in a short skirt batted her eyes at him.

"Here, let me get that," said Alex, leaping for the front door. "It's usually open."

"That's not very safe." Sara stepped over the threshold and paused, waiting for a greeting, but all she heard was the faint sound of canned laughter downstairs, and demented "music" upstairs. An axe murderer could waltz in and chop up her grandchildren, and no one would notice. Alex set Sara's bag at the bottom of the stairs where anyone could trip over it.

"Thank you," she said, inviting him to leave.

"I think I'll say hello to the girls," he said. "Maggie, come down! Grandma is home!" he shouted, sauntering toward the back of the house.

Alex certainly seemed comfortable here. She would have to speak to Meredith about that.

Examining her nail polish as if it were the Rosetta Stone, Maggie skulked down from her lair. Once she would have run to her grandmother and hurled herself at her legs, but that was a long time ago, before the divorce and adolescence made her surly. Who could blame her? She had too much responsibility, minding Lucy and herself, cooking dinner some nights, trying to keep up with her own schoolwork and misguided fashion trends. Sara took hold of the banister, and Maggie did give her a very nice hug.

"I'm glad you're better, Grandma," she said. Well, Meredith had done a decent job with the girls, the best she could given the difficulties Alex had inflicted on them all.

"Hello, Sweetheart," Sara said. "I don't think I'm contagious, but I'm not going to kiss you, just in case. How are you doing? I hardly got to see you before your mother hurried me off to the hospital."

"I'm fine," said Maggie. "I think you needed to go. They kept you a couple days."

"They always keep old people. They just want the Medicare money. Hello, Lucy," she said, as Alex came back holding her hand. When she saw Sara, Lucy hurried up and threw her arms around her waist.

"Grandma," Lucy crooned. Sara was truly touched. Meredith may not be much in the housekeeping department, but she was raising some very good girls.

"You're both so tall. I swear you've grown several inches since Thanksgiving." She took their arms, and they strolled into the living room together and sat down on the couch.

"Sara, would you like some tea?" Alex asked.

"Yes, thank you. But I'm sure Maggie can fix it so you can go back to work."

"No, I cancelled the rest of my appointments. I'm all yours. In fact, I might even make dinner," he said.

"Yay," said Lucy. "Cheesy spaghetti!"

"Big whoop," said Maggie.

"I don't know what that will do to my stomach," said Sara. "I'm sure I can make something healthier." She attempted to stand, but the soft couch cushions gave her no leverage, and she plopped back down.

"Nonsense," said Alex. "I'll get your tea, and then I'll rustle up some grub for all my best girls. Lucy, why don't you help me. Maggie, you stay and keep your grandma company."

As Lucy sashayed into the kitchen, Sara squeezed Maggie's bare thigh. "So, tell me how you really are," Sara said. "I want the straight scoop."

"I'm fine," Maggie said. She touched her grandmother's hand with one finger.

"I miss you, you know," said Sara.

"You just saw us a couple days ago," Maggie said. Then she met Sara's eyes. "I miss you too," she said, and looked down at the coffee table.

"It was nice when I lived in Evanston, and I could see you all the time."

Sara had lived in Kansas City for years, but when Maggie was born and Meredith wanted to work part time, Sara moved to Evanston to help out. At first she had worried about leaving familiar

48

surroundings, but many of her friends had already migrated to warmer climates or to be near their own grandchildren. For a while, the move was wonderful. When Meredith had to stay late at work, Sara could pop in and take care of her grandbabies, give them dinner and baths and tuck them into bed. She watched their Halloween parades and attended all of their birthday parties, and a few of their soccer games, if it wasn't too chilly and damp outside. But as she neared seventy, the cold winters bothered her more, and living on the North Shore was slippery and expensive. Life would be healthier in Florida, she thought, and she did enjoy her new friends in Independence Valley, An Active Retirement Community, despite the degrading round of petting zoos and bingo games the director provided for entertainment. But she missed her family. Soon Maggie and Lucy would go to college. Sara wondered if they would ever visit her then, after they grew up.

Alex returned with a mug of hot tea, and Lucy set an unopened package of Vienna Fingers on the coffee table next to it. "Thank you, Lucy. I don't know if we should eat these now. They might spoil our dinner."

"That's okay, Grandma," said Lucy. "Everybody hates them except you."

"Even your mother?" asked Sara. She had always bought them for Meredith when she was growing up.

"Yup," said Lucy. "Mom says they're old lady cookies. No offense," she tossed back, leaving the room.

"You don't like them either, Maggie?" Sara asked.

"Mom bought them for you."

"That was very thoughtful," said Sara. "I suppose I'm company now. I remember when I was just part of the family. I used to take care of you quite a bit. Do you remember that?"

"Sure, I remember," said Maggie. "You were great. Kind of like Mom, but calmer."

"When you were very little, you used to put your hands on both sides of my head and say, 'I like your hair, Grandma.' It was so sweet. Do you remember that?"

"Not really," said Maggie.

Life could be so sad, Sara thought. She had poured so much energy and love into Maggie and Lucy, but she doubted they remembered much of that now. And then, right before Alex's bombshell, when they needed her most, Sara had moved to Florida. Meredith had insisted that they were fine, that she could take care of the girls and herself, and that Sara should enjoy the balmy winters, she deserved it. Meredith was independent, and that was as it should be. But now Maggie was a teenager, and Lucy was almost twelve. Some people said that was a danger zone, that teenagers need the most monitoring and stability, and Sara knew that her daughter's oversight hadn't always been what it should be. And now, Alex seemed to be circling.

Sara heard the back door rattle. A few moments later, Meredith, in stocking feet and carrying a worn briefcase, wandered into the living room.

"Hello Mom," she said, leaning in for a kiss.

"Don't kiss me," said Sara. "I don't want to make you sick."

"I called your room, but you were gone. I would have picked you up." Meredith walked into the hallway and dropped her briefcase by the front closet.

"I know, Honey, but I didn't want to bother you."

"It was nice of Alex to bring you."

"I suppose," said Sara. "He seems to want to be here."

"He does." Meredith flushed.

"I was thinking," said Sara, "that I might extend my visit after all. I'm not sure I should be flying with my lungs in this condition. And I could help out with the girls."

"Dinner is ready," Alex announced, entering the room. "As soon as you slip into something more comfortable," he said, turning to Meredith.

"Of course, Mom. Whatever you think. We would love to have you."

"Good. I'll call the airlines tonight. Maggie, Lucy, give your old granny a boost." They each took an elbow and hoisted her off the couch. "Let's go into the dining room and see what your father has cooked up this time," she said.

Chapter Six

Why would anyone live in the ravines, Cece wondered, spiraling into the Hades that Ellen and Mason called home. She acknowledged the dramatic landscape, a forested descent into a lace-limbed gulch, the lake shimmering off a bluff to the east. But the road swerved like a serpent, tricky now, in June, and death-defying in winter, when the road was pocked with potholes and veiled in black ice and blinded with a hedge of snow.

"Mom, I feel sick. I need to go home," said Clara, pressing one hand against the tummy of her pink polo shirt and the other over her mouth.

"It's all this zig-zagging. Open your window," said Cece. "We're almost there."Accelerating out of the ravines, Cece turned left onto Scott Road and parked. "When was the last time you ate something?"

"I don't know. I think I had some gummy bears this morning? Oh, yeah. And a bottle of Evian."

Cece didn't want to criticize – no telling what eating disorder a girl might develop if her mother started dissecting her food choices. And Clara did look lovely, so tall and slender. "Well, I'm sure Ellen will have some carrot sticks to tide you over until dinner. Let's go."

Stutter-stepping down the narrow shoulder of Sheridan Road, Cece, in a pencil skirt and kitten heels, concentrated on her footing. If they weren't going to provide proper sidewalks, at least the village could sweep up the forest rubble that had settled in her path. Thank goodness Ellen's house was near the ravines' northern edge, so they didn't have to hike too far. Now the one lane road, which headed up and disappeared, loomed in front of her.

Yards ahead in flat, strappy sandals, Clara turned and walked backwards up the asphalt. "I bet they're not even home," she said.

"Don't be silly," said Cece. "Are you feeling any better?"

"A little."

They finally reached the top. The house, a boxy contemporary of bleached natural wood, blended with the forest on the west and sank several stories down the cliff on the lake side. It was spectacular, if you liked that sort of thing, and Cece wondered how Ellen and Mason could afford it. She doubted that Sanford had helped them, she couldn't imagine why he would. Ellen undoubtedly earned more than she was worth, and Mason probably lucked into some good investments. And they surely bought at a bargain price – few Winnetkans would want such a modern house. It was hardly a homey place to raise children, which Ellen and Mason didn't have in any case, no surprise.

They hurried along a stone walk with vined walls looming on both sides. Pressing the doorbell, Cece smoothed her hair, waited, and pushed again.

She felt sweaty and disheveled after all that climbing and badly wanted to freshen up.

Mason opened the door. A green chef's apron stamped "Dartmouth" covered his small potbelly. His stubby fingers raked fly-away strands of graying hair over an advancing bald spot and pushed up his glasses.

"Please come in," he said. "Alan is on the deck, and Jessica is setting the table. Ellen should be here shortly, she was delayed at work. Please, walk through. Would you care for a beverage?"

Cece stared at a decorative white metal projectile dangling from the cathedral ceiling, and then through the living room at the wall of windows facing the lake. The wood floors were stained a slate gray, and the scant rectangular furniture was upholstered in dove leather. A telescope next to the windows would permit Ellen to watch sailors flail next to their capsized boats from the sterility of her home.

"Where is the lady's room?" asked Cece.

Mason pointed left into the kitchen – plain-faced charcoal cabinets, an enormous granite island, and floors that appeared to be polished cement. Next to the island, Jessica, in a floral smocked jumper that did her no favors, stood sipping a Waterford balloon glass brimming with white wine.

"Hello!" she said brightly. "I'm hostess while Mason grills and Ellen drives home. Please, have some cheese and crackers. Would you like a drink?"

"A glass of Chardonnay for me please. And a Perrier for Clara." Cece nodded toward the appetizers, and Clara cautiously approached a Triscuit. Unable to spot a restroom, Cece eyed the kitchen sink, but turning on the sleek, curved faucet appeared to be impossible. She grabbed her wine and took a large swig.

"So sorry I'm late," Ellen said, bursting into the kitchen through a panel that turned out to be a door to the garage. She dropped her briefcase and tugged off her jacket. As she aged, Ellen looked increasingly like her mother, if April had taken care of herself. With her sleek, dark hair and pixie size, it was hard to believe that sandy, distinguished Sanford had any input into her gene pool at all. Ellen smoothed her skirt and licked her lips. "I am parched. Is there anything to drink?" She turned her back on Jessica, who wordlessly poured a large glass of Cabernet.

"Perfect timing." Mason stepped through the glass door from the deck. Alan followed, toting one bottle of beer and grabbing another. "The steaks are ready."

"Rare and bloody, I hope," said Ellen, wine bottle in one hand and glass in the other.

Jessica handed Mason a beer. "For the chef," she said. Cradling the salad bowl, she took a chug from her goblet and followed everyone onto the deck.

All they had to eat was gross raw meat and oily crouton salad that made her feel like hurling. Ever since her father lay shot in the park next door, Clara hadn't been able to eat anything red and oozing. Usually she grabbed a bowl of Special K and a Twizzler and called it dinner, but Ellen and Mason obviously specialized in food that had been screaming for its life two seconds before it appeared on their plates. Jessica wasn't eating her steak either, but she made up for it gorging on salad dissolved in an acid bath of alcohol. Actually, everyone at the table, including her mother, was drinking like they had sidled up to the last open bar on earth. Clara crunched an ice cube and dispersed her meal to the four corners of her plate. Trust Ellen to have square dishes. Everything about her was edgy.

"So, why are we here, anyway?" Clara was grumpy from starvation, and the grown-ups being fake polite was getting really old. She expected her mother to correct her manners, but Cece just sat there, swilling her wine and waiting for the answer. Ellen calmly chewed a chunk of rubbery meat, while Mason looked puffy and flustered, as if the stick up his ass had just inflated.

Resting her fork on her plate, Ellen swallowed and addressed Clara. "After I left your house the other day, I started to think. I mean, with Dad gone so suddenly, it does make a philosophical person aware of her own mortality and of what's really important in life. Alan and I had quite a nice talk about this, and we realized that the most important thing in the world is love – love for friends, love for family."

"It's all you need," offered Mason.

"Exactly," said Ellen. "And Clara, we realized that you aren't going to be around much longer. I mean, you'll be going to college in another year. You've always been so much the baby of the family, Alan and I have been remiss about including you in our lives. But we want to make up for lost time. Isn't that right, Alan?"

Alan lifted his beer bottle toward Clara and nodded. "We want to get to know you better, Sis," he said. "And you too, Um," he added, swiveling toward Cece.

"Exactly," said Ellen. "And I was also thinking, watching Mason struggling to deal with Dad's legacy …."

"Which I'm glad to do for you, Mom, it's no problem," said Mason.

"She's not your mom," said Clara. "Can I have a drink?"

"As I was saying," Ellen said, ignoring Clara and refilling everyone else's wine glass, "It's still hard for me to believe that Dad died without a will. But there it is. Which made me realize that Mason and I don't have wills either. Do you have wills, Alan and Jessica?"

"Why, no we don't," said Alan, as Jessica emptied the salad bowl onto her plate. "What about you?" asked Alan, turning to Cece. "You must have a will, with Clara here. In case anything ever happened to you. I mean – you must have designated someone to take care of her."

"I don't recall being asked," said Ellen.

"I just wrote it on a piece of paper," said Cece. "Anyway, it doesn't matter anymore. Clara is an adult now."

"So you didn't leave all your worldly possessions to the dog and cat hospital, nothing like that," said Ellen.

"Nobody asked me if I have a will," said Clara.

"Do you?" asked Alan.

"That's for me to know and you to find out," said Clara.

"Spoken like a true adult," said Ellen.

"I feel sick," said Jessica. She pushed back her chair and stumbled into the house.

"Excuse us," said Alan.

The phone started to ring in the kitchen. "That might be the office," said Ellen, standing up. She hurried through the open deck door.

Clara gave her mother a look, but Cece appeared to have detached from her surroundings. She was staring past the treetops to the blue of the lake. "It's lovely here," Cece murmured. "The last light is so precious, soft, with just a hint of chill in the air. It's true, Sanford's death has made me think about my life. I've always been drawn to the water, but I never go to the lake, I never walk along the beach. It's wonderful, having your own bit of shoreline. A little slice of heaven."

"We should go down there," said Clara.

"I don't really have the right shoes," said Cece.

"Next time," said Mason, standing up, and starting to clear the dishes. "No, no, you're our guest," he said, as Cece half-heartedly waved her hand over Jessica's plate.

Clara grabbed her water glass and followed her mother and Mason into the kitchen. Sighing, she set her glass on the island, lit like an operating table, and fingered the scalpel-sharp chef's knife resting on the cutting board next to the dregs of a tomato. She wondered if vegetables screamed, a pitch inaudible to humans but searing to other plants, when ripped from a vine or sliced to be eaten. Anything was possible.

The floor was made of atoms, it was full of holes that she couldn't see, and she didn't fall through it – but the holes were there. The world was kind of creepy, if you thought about it too much.

Ellen, who had reassembled herself as Barbie, Attorney for the Damned while on the phone, returned it to its cradle and pushed the panel which opened to the garage. "So sorry, duty calls. Lovely to see you all, thanks for coming."

"Thank you," said Cece. "We'll be leaving in a moment too." Ellen grabbed her briefcase and dashed out to her car.

Mopping her chin and her Mary Poppins jumper, Jessica returned from the powder room and pulled another panel, to reveal the innards of a refrigerator. "I brought cheesecake," she said, setting a giant, lemony pill garnished with whipped cream and gelatinous strawberries the size of apples, in the center of the island. "Who would like a slice?" Brandishing a carving knife, she deposited a burp in the palm of her left hand.

"Let's get you home," said Alan, retrieving the knife and setting it on the counter. "Thanks, Mason. Great to see you."

"Yes, thank you," said Jessica, leaning her cheek against his.

"I think we should be going too," said Clara. "I have that badminton thingy. Mom."

"Yes, of course," said Cece. "Just let me go to the ladies for a moment. It's this way?"

As Cece wobbled around the corner, Clara trailed her finger around the cheesecake and hoped her mother would be able to find the toilet. Mason marched in and out, clearing dirty dishes from the deck. As he retied his college apron, Cece returned. "Thank you for having us, Mason. And thank you for helping me with Sanford's finances. I appreciate your expertise."

"Glad to be of assistance," said Mason.

"I feel terrible leaving you with this mess." Cece shrugged helplessly.

"Nonsense. I'm sorry Ellen had to rush off."

"It is Monday," said Cece, walking to the front door. "I understand. Thanks again."

"Thank you for coming." Mason bowed. "I'll be in touch."

Mason escorted them to the front door and opened it. Clara and her mother stepped out into the cool evening air. The light had dimmed from a glow to dusk, and while Clara could still see when they were near the house, once they were among the trees at the bottom of the ravine, it was hard to find their way along the narrow, cluttered path next to the street.

"Let's cross and walk on the left, facing oncoming traffic," said Cece. "That will be safer."

"Yeah, whatever."

Cece asserted positions as if they were facts, and Clara felt it was her job to quibble. But she followed her mother across the street. You had to pick your battles, Cece used to say when talking to Sanford about Clara. Clara liked that view, it let her parents spoil her. They were pretty great parents, they loved her a lot. Clara always knew she was loved.

"I learned that in Girl Scouts," Cece said, skirting a tree branch.

"What, did you get a merit badge in walking on the side of the road?"

"You don't get a merit badge for everything you do," said Cece, rounding a curve.

The headlights were so bright, blinding in the darkness of the ravine. They shone full on Cece, picking her way gamely along, a few feet ahead of Clara. Cece reared and tried to back up, but there was no escape, the hill next to them rose up too steep. Clara saw her mother throw her arms out in front of her, as if she could stop the car with her pink-manicured fingertips. There was barely time to scream as the car hit them both, swerved, and then barreled south through the ravines, toward the city.

Often during the course of their marriage, Alex worked late at Evanston Hospital, or said he did, and Shawna had to eat dinner alone. She would open a plastic bag of salad and dump it in a bowl with some torn lunch meat, or reheat last night's chicken in the microwave and flip through the latest *Cosmo* article on bedtime tricks that will blow your man's mind. That's when she hated her life most. But she didn't realize how good she had it then until now, when she tried to eat with a baby in the house. According to what she could remember about evolution from high school biology, Lex should want her to eat so that she could feed him, but it was increasingly clear that babies knew nothing about what was good for them. Lex was a time bomb set to explode whenever she lifted a fork to her mouth. Shawna had been home alone with Lex for two solid days, ever since Alex picked her up at the hospital, dumped her back in

Kenilworth, and skulked off to his bachelor pad. And all Lex did was cry.

Lex cried so much. He cried when he was hungry and when he was tired, when she changed his diaper and when she didn't. She was too scared to give him a bath, she might scald or freeze or drown him. Trying to change his clothes – well, forget it, he wouldn't stick his arm through the hole, and his head hung limp like a bud on a broken stem. And the navy blue nub of his navel, and his wee circumcision, which probably stung – nobody told her she needed a nursing degree just to survive the first week.

If Alex would move back in and help her, even just at night, she thought she could manage. It might even be fun, though she doubted it. How was she supposed to survive with no sleep and no food and this thing that hated her screaming all the time? Shawna yanked a slice of pizza out of the fridge, jammed the cold point into her mouth, and gnawed it leaning over the counter, like an animal.

Through the kitchen window, she could see the Whitakers' house next door. Yesterday, Cece had offered to help Shawna, and she seemed sincere, but the house was dark. Cece was probably gallivanting around at some benefit, her diamond earrings twinkling as she smiled above a fresh, hot steak at the witty chat of the man to her left. Mashed potatoes. Or maybe she was crouched in the twilight, weeping at her husband's grave, watering the little sprigs of grass just emerging from the mound over his body, if shot men were allowed to get buried in cemeteries on the North Shore. He might still be in a drawer somewhere, as evidence for when the police admitted he was murdered and caught his killer. Because, face it, no adult is dumb enough to take a gun to the park and accidentally shoot himself, no matter what the Kenilworth Chamber of Commerce wanted everybody to believe.

Gnawing a second pizza slice, Shawna checked the front and back doors. She had never felt safe alone in this house at night. The streets were poorly lit, which was supposed to be charming, but just struck her as creepy. And the houses sat on big lots, not acres like farmland, but roomy enough that, if something bad happened, nobody would hear it – hell, nobody heard the gunshot in the park that day. And everybody knew that Kenilworth was, like, the richest town around. If you were some poor, angry criminal from the South Side with your mind set on the biggest possible haul of jewelry and stock certificates, and on a revenge rape and murder because you had to live in the slums in a food desert and take the el, you could do worse than to come to Kenilworth and break into a house like this one, with a new VCR and a lactating sitting duck. Maybe they would even take Lex and demand a ransom, with a piece of loose leaf paper with letters cut out from the *Sun Times*.

Wiping grease from her mouth with the back of her hand, Shawna thought she heard something, a scraping sound like a man trying to jimmy her living room window with a switchblade. She heard the scrape again, and she entered the living room, but she didn't dare go near the window and peer through it, in case someone stared back and she totally lost her mind. Frozen in the dim glow from the kitchen, she couldn't turn on a lamp, because then he would see her, and even though she wasn't looking her best, in sweat pants and Alex's old college tee shirt with a crust of spit-up on the shoulder, the rapist/murderer wouldn't see the spit-up, just the fact that she was a young blonde woman all alone. Backing up, she tripped and tipped over the stupid car seat that Lex preferred to his expensive baby beds, and which she forgot was there, and Lex dumped out, and she almost fell on top of him, and they both started to cry.

The phone was ringing. Shawna rubbed her leg and wiped her eyes and picked up the baby, because that is what mothers do, they put their babies first, even when their babies try to kill them by booby-trapping their escape route and blowing their cover. Maybe Alex was calling to check on her, maybe right this minute he was on his way over to visit his son and namesake and to keep his eye on things so that she could finally get some sleep.

"Hello," she said, but she couldn't hear anything because Lex was screaming so loud. "Just a minute," she said, and she marched Lex upstairs, set him in his crib, and shut the door. She went back downstairs and picked up the phone. She could hardly hear Lex now. She should have thought of this before. "Yes, hello," she said, but no one answered, the phone was dead.

Shawna hung up. Maybe someone was checking to see if she was home, maybe someone with evil purposes, who wanted her to be there. She went into the kitchen, where all she could hear was the rhythmic kerplunk of perfect crescents falling out of the automatic icemaker. She pulled a giant knife, probably meant for butchering large animals like deer or wild turkeys, and which she normally avoided for fear of amputating a hand, from the block on the counter, and stood with her back to the refrigerator for a few minutes. When the icemaker noise stopped, she could hear the scraping again, and faintly Lex, but that was all. No one was coming into the house, at least not yet.

She felt a painful stinging in her breasts and a warm dribble down her stomach and into the waistband of her pants. Of course, her milk had come in. She blotted herself, and a wet, sticky stain spread across the front of her tee shirt from both sides. She was a cow, a fat, smelly, cow, her body was disgusting. No one was going to break in, no one would want to get that close to her. Summoning her courage, she walked back into the living room, leaned over the sofa, and pressed her face against the window, where a twig from a miniature lilac bush blew back and forth against the glass.

Now she could hear Lex shrieking, a shrill, gurgling vibrato. She imagined a cartoon baby, its mouth as wide as the entrance to hell, its tonsils shivering like a punching bag. Still carrying the knife, she walked upstairs to his room, the nursery that she had so lovingly decorated, with attention to every fluffy chick and moon and star, and which he so clearly hated. He hated her too. And why shouldn't he? She was stinking livestock who didn't know how to take care of him properly, and who couldn't keep his father away from the homely old bat he had divorced and make him want to stay and love his son. She was at the door of the nursery now, and the crying was so loud, a scream of sorrow and anger that would never, ever stop.

Shawna opened the door and walked across the handmade rug to the crib. Switching the knife to her left hand, she turned on the magic forest lamp, a glow that cast revolving shadows of trees and birds flying around the walls and over the ceiling. The knife clutched tight, she stepped close to the crib and looked into it.

There was a baby, they said it was hers. He was angry, demonic, his arms and legs flailing, his face pinched and red and soaking wet. But as she stared at him, the monster in her mind began to shrink, and she realized how small he was in the crib, and how helpless. In his fury or despair, he had maneuvered himself into a corner, his head wedged against a satin bumper pad, his legs wheeling like a bug on its back. He barely filled a tenth of the crib, he was just a tiny ball with little fists pounding the air, not even stirring up a breeze. Noticing the knife, she walked across the room and set it on the dresser behind a stuffed rabbit. Then Shawna went back and picked up her baby and held him. He began to knock his face and snuggle against her chest, and she knew what he wanted. Cradling him, she eased into the chair and pulled up her shirt. As Shawna pumped her heels up and down to rock them both, Lex snorted, sighed, and began to nurse.

Chapter Seven

It was Tuesday morning, a chilly, drizzling Chicago June day. Traffic-court ready in a gray pantsuit and sensible shoes, Meredith found her mother resting on the sunroom couch with the TV on mute. In a purple velour track suit and fuzzy slippers, with a magazine of crossword puzzles to her left, the remote control and a box of Kleenex to her right, and a cup of tea and a saucer of toast rinds on the table in front of her, Sara looked like a retired general holed up in her tent for the duration of the war.

"How are you feeling, Mom? I can stay home if you need me." Meredith peered at her mother, who looked smaller and whiter than usual.

"Don't be silly," Sara said, trying to straighten up. "I worry about you, always taking care of everyone else, going to work and then doing everything for your girls. You know, Maggie had a big bowl of ice cream last night, and she just left her dish in the sink, as if some maid were going to clean it up."

"That was me, Mom. And please do ask them to help you while I'm gone."

"Oh, I don't need help." Sara paused to cough and shakily reach for her tea. "I'm just thinking about

67

dinnertime, when you get home. It's such a rush for you." Sara frowned. "We could order Chinese, but take-out is always so gloppy."

Somehow, her mother's concern always left Meredith with the same burdens, but slathered with a thick layer of guilt. If she took some chicken out of the freezer, she could broil that, and with a little rice and a salad, they would have a reasonable family meal. And, to prove that she wasn't a bad mother who failed to instill a sense of responsibility into her children, she would make Maggie dump the salad into the bowl.

On the television, an inaudible anchorwoman in a spandex dress was reading the local news. Over her shoulder, a screen displayed a photo of a road in a wooded area, and then of a well-groomed older woman who looked disturbingly familiar.

"Mom, could you turn up the sound?" Meredith dove for the remote as she realized that, by the time Sara noodled out that bit of electronic wizardry, the station would have moved to a commercial for breakfast cereal. Tape of Winnetka Police Officer Joe Malone, a Channel 7 microphone in his face, now filled the screen.

"The victims were attempting to exit the ravine on foot at approximately 8:00 p.m. They appear to have been walking northbound on the southbound shoulder of Sheridan Road, when an unknown vehicle struck them. The vehicle failed to stop and left the scene of the accident." Officer Malone reported this in a professional monotone, as if finding bodies strewn around the streets of Winnetka were a common occupational hazard.

The screen then switched back to the anchorwoman. "Kenilworth resident Cece Whitaker was pronounced dead at the scene. Her daughter Clara was taken by ambulance to Evanston Hospital, where she remains in stable condition. Her injuries do not appear to be life threatening. Anyone with information is asked to call the Winnetka Police."

"That's terrible," said Sara, shaking her head, as a trio of Frosted Flakes danced across the screen, and Meredith muted it again. "That poor family. And someone just hit them and left them there, like garbage. Really, it's unimaginable." Sara reached for a tissue and blew her nose. "I don't understand how people can be so callous."

"They panic." In her thirteen years as a Cook County prosecutor, Meredith had seen her share of hit-and-runs. "They're trying to protect themselves – they were driving drunk or didn't have a license, or they were kids and don't want their parents to get mad. If they keep going, maybe they won't get caught, or magically maybe it won't have happened. I can't believe it – I just met that woman two days ago. She's Shawna's next door neighbor. Her husband died in April. He shot himself accidentally."

"He shot himself, and then she got hit by a car. That's a lot of bad luck for one family. That poor girl. She's an orphan now."

Sara was right, that was a real bad luck streak. If this were a Greek tragedy, the Winnetka police force would circle Clara's hospital bed to bemoan the curse on the House of Whitaker, and further inquiry would reveal that Clara's great grandfather had served his nephews to their father for dinner. Meredith decided to suspend judgment while the Winnetka Police did their job.

"Do you want any more tea, before I go? Any juice?"

"No, I'm fine, but what about you? Aren't you going to eat anything?"

Meredith picked up Sara's plate of toast crusts. "I'll grab something on the way."

"Black coffee and a chocolate doughnut is no way to start the day. You need to take care of your health. How long could it take to make a scrambled egg and a slice of wheat toast?"

"How did you know it would be chocolate?" Meredith stared at her mother. Sometimes her powers of perception were a bit unnerving.

"I've know you longer than you've known yourself," said Sara. "And don't you ever forget it."

From: mason.Humphrey@fidelitysecurity.com
To: ewhitaker@winters.com
Re: last night
Date: June 9, 1998

Hi Ellen,
I wanted to make sure you are okay. I assume you have been working. Did you hear about Cece and Clara's accident? Cece is dead and Clara is at Evanston Hospital. It's a terrible thing. Now my work on Sanford's estate has doubled, because everything that belonged to Cece will go to Clara, as her only child.

I know you are busy, but it might make sense for you to go visit Clara in the hospital. She is your sister, and now she is alone. We can help her with her finances and other plans.

I feel sorry if our barbecue contributed to Cece's death in any way. I am glad you were well on your way downtown by the time of the accident.

Love,
Mason

From: ewhitaker@winters.com
To: mason.Humphrey@fidelitysecurity.com
Re: last night
Date: June 9, 1998

Dear Mason,
I am fine. I have a lot of work to do. I didn't see anything unusual in the ravines on my way downtown. I am so sorry about Cece and Clara. I will visit Clara today and extend our best wishes for her speedy recovery.

As these terrible things happen, I greatly appreciate your support. I will see you tonight.

Love,
Ellen

Clara had never even visited a hospital room before. Once, in a rush to finish a coloring project before kindergarten, she had catapulted down the basement stairs of their old house in Kenilworth. When she landed, screaming, on the cement floor, her forearm crooked, Cece rushed her to the emergency room. Even then, she had returned home the same day. Her father, of course, had done all of his dying in the fresh air. And, whether from hearty genes or an act of will, her mother was never sick. Cece was always there.

Clara kept sliding toward the pit of her pleated bed and then struggling to sit up without gouging her scraped arms into the mattress. Every hour, a nurse yanked a blood pressure cuff from the wall, Velcroed it around her arm, and inflated it until she cried with pain. Another nurse had stuck an I.V. into a vein in Clara's hand and taped it over the bruise on her wrist. When she wanted to use the toilet, she had to call someone to wheel the pole hung with a plastic bag attached to her by a rubber tube, while she tried to keep her hospital gown from flapping open in the back. An aide had drawn a half dozen tubes of bright red blood in the middle of the night and then reappeared with a tray of gelatinous breakfast that she wouldn't have touched even if her stomach weren't up in her throat.

Everyone who came into her room looked scared, and no one told her anything. A TV on the wall spewed pictures of game show hosts in loud jackets with flashing lights and valuable prizes, but no sound came out of anything or anyone except the old woman in bed behind a curtain, who moaned and shuffled by to use their shared facilities. Water

72

seeped from Clara's eyes, but she felt as if the loneliness and fear that overflowed from them belonged to some other girl, a girl who didn't live the normal life of a New Trier senior, but instead struggled somewhere dangerous in Chicago and then appeared on the inside pages of the *Tribune* in a one paragraph article about being left for dead in the back alley of a bad neighborhood that Clara would never, ever see.

She heard a tap on the half-closed door of her room, and then the tentative rustle of dry-cleaned suits, as Ellen and Alan shuffled in to stand awkwardly over her. "How are you?" asked Ellen. "You look better than I thought you would. Though," she added, glancing at Clara's arms and chest, "I'm not sure I'd enter the Miss Teen Illinois contest just yet."

"I'm okay," said Clara. "What are you doing here? Don't you have work or something?" She tried to pull herself upright, to be at less of a disadvantage. "Ow."

"Here," said Alan, "what can I do?"

"I don't know," said Clara. "I want to see my mom. Where is she? Is she down the hall?"

Ellen and Alan looked at each other. A nurse came in with a thermometer and headed for the blood pressure cuff. "Hello," said Alan. "We're Clara's brother and sister. Could we speak to you for a minute outside?"

They left, and Clara sank back into her crooked pillows, all of which hit her at awkward, uncomfortable places on her neck and spine. Her brother and sister – very funny, not. They never gave a hoot about her – if she had died in the accident last night, they would probably be glad. They had always resented her, because their father loved her most. And who cares, they were adults, they shouldn't need their father, not the way Clara did. Now Sanford was gone. But Ellen had Mason, and Alan had Jessica, and if they wanted younger friends, they could have their own children, icky thought. And Clara had her mother. She wished she had her father too, but she always had her mother.

Ellen and Alan came back in. Ellen was wearing a business outfit, a fluffy white blouse and a fitted navy skirt and jacket that made her look thin. Alan wore a maroon tie and a starched shirt with gross sweat spots under the arms. His forehead was up in his hairline with fake concern, but Ellen looked like she was calculating the tip for an expensive meal. A crisp mommish woman with a clipboard and clicking high heels tapped around Ellen and Alan, yanked a plastic chair close to Clara's bed, and perched.

"Hello, Clara. I'm Mrs. Keene, the hospital social worker. How are you doing today?"

Clara cautiously accepted the Kleenex box that Mrs. Whatever shoved in her direction. Clara knew some kids who skipped class to sit in a circle with the school social worker and talk meaningfully about their parents' divorces, and she knew one girl who went to a therapist once a week for an eating disorder. She didn't know why this lady was here, but Clara certainly wasn't about to tell a total stranger in a polyester blouse a damn thing.

"I'm in the hospital," said Clara. "How are you?"

"I'm fine, thank you for asking. I've talked to your doctor, and he thinks you might be ready to go home today. We want to make sure you are discharged to a safe place."

Clara narrowed her eyes. "I've got a nice house in Kenilworth. Where's my mother? Does she have to stay here? I can take care of myself."

"Yes, well. As you know, your mother was hit by the car that hit you last night." The lady paused. Clara waited. "Her injuries were worse than yours. In fact, they were quite serious." She stopped again. Clara closed her eyes. "I'm afraid, Dear, that by the time she got to the hospital last night, your mother was too far gone for us to help her. I'm so sorry."

Clara squeezed her eyes shut, but tears streamed out anyway, and she clutched her sheets and emitted a long, low groan that accelerated into a shriek. Every nerve in her body sparked, and she felt unreal, like she was a cartoon of a burning flash floating a foot above her bed. Time stopped, and then she felt nothing, not the pain from her bruises, not the tug of the I.V. line as she thrashed around the bed. The nurse must have come back, because there was a needle, and then she sank back and the sounds stopped. But her arms and legs trembled, and her face steamed, red hot and wet. As the room spun, Clara remembered being sick as a little girl, the uncontrollable shivering, her fiery cheeks, and the walls moving towards her as the bed spun in space. Her mother had brought her ginger ale and changed her sheets, so that the bed felt cool and clean, and she read her stories and held her hand until she slept. She needed her mother to comfort her, to tell her that she was safe. She needed her mother to tell her that it was okay that she was dead.

Ellen moved to the other side of the bed and stared into her face. "Don't worry," she said. "Alan and Mason and I will take care of everything. We'll handle the funeral and figure out your financial situation. We can take care of everything," she repeated.

"You just need to focus on getting well," added Alan. "You're lucky, you have lawyers and a financial planner to look out for your interests. You don't have to worry about a thing."

"I don't want your help," mumbled Clara. "She was my mother, not yours. Stay away from us."

Mrs. Keene glanced between Ellen and Alan. "The pressing situation at the moment is discharging Clara to a safe place. Is either of you willing to take care of her during her recovery? We don't want her popping back here with an infection."

"Of course," said Ellen. "She can stay with me for as long as necessary. My husband and I would be delighted to have her."

"Forget it," muttered Clara. "I'm not going with her. I'm an adult, I have a house. It's my house. I have money. I have a lot of money. I have friends. You can't make me go with them."

"You don't know what you're saying." Ellen turned to Mrs. Keene. "She doesn't know what she's saying. She's crazy with grief."

Mrs. Keene stood up. "Well, it seems to me that Clara has family and resources. And frankly, her injuries aren't particularly serious. I'm sure she'll be fine. We do want you to come to terms with your loss, Clara. You have until the end of the day. Oh, and about your mother's remains and personal effects

– I understand from your sister that you are your mother's next of kin."

"Yes," said Clara.

"We'll give you her things before you go. Is there a funeral home you would like me to call?

"Yes," said Clara weakly. "Donellan, please. They took care of my father." She started to cry again.

There was a quiet knocking at the door, almost a scratching, more like a small rodent than a nurse. The door eased open, and Jessica tip-toed into the room. Her face was white and puffy, her cheeks snaked with damp streaks of eyeliner and pink blush. Her hands fluttering, she walked uncertainly to the foot of the bed.

"I'm so sorry, Clara," she said. "How are you feeling?"

Alan moved to his wife and took her arm. "Honey, you didn't need to come." He turned to the social worker. "She's so soft-hearted," he explained.

"Well, you all work it out," said Mrs. Keene, as her pager beeped and she left.

"Clara wants us all to leave," said Alan, steering Jessica toward the door. "She needs to rest now."

"But look, she's crying," said Jessica. "We can't go now." Jessica walked over to Clara and sat in the empty chair beside her.

"Well, I have to go to work," said Ellen. "I think you're making a mistake, Clara. We can look out for your interests."

"Get out," said Clara. "I want everyone out."

"I'll talk to you when you're lucid," said Ellen.

"Get her out of here!" cried Clara. She picked up her Styrofoam water cup and threw it, but it arced and landed on the floor next to the bed.

"Come on, Ellen," said Alan, grabbing her arm. "You too, Honey," he said, touching Jessica's shoulder.

"Are you sure, Clara? I'll just sit quietly. I won't say a word. I just want to do something for you." Jessica started to sob. Clara turned her face away. "Let us take care of you," Jessica said. Clara closed her eyes.

"I think she needs to rest. Goodbye, Clara. Call me later, and I'll drive you home," said Alan. "Okay, everyone, let's let her sleep. She's had a shock."

Clara listened for the sound of her horrible quasi-family's receding footsteps. It would be a cold day in hell before she called any of them for anything. She would find someone else to help her. A nurse came in, and Clara heard moaning. The nurse pulled back her neighbor's curtain, but no one was there.

As he stepped off the elevator, the odor of onions and cumin and the sting of an exotic pepper smacked Alex and sent him scurrying to his own front door. His hallway neighbor, a fresh divorcee, must be entertaining the chick-de-jour with his newfound expertise in international cooking. Alex didn't know whether to be jealous or disgusted, but he did know he didn't like the stench. Slamming the front door, he sighed in relief, and then in sadness, at the sterility of his own home of the last few months.

At first, the view of the lake from the fourth floor had overcome the depressing old-ladyness of the rest of the place. And he figured he wouldn't be there long. Meredith would realize that she wanted him back, and then they would find a new house exactly like the house in Kenilworth that they had owned before he met Shawna and blew up their marriage. Paying for two houses might make money a little tight, but surely Shawna would want to downsize. She was just rattling around in their giant cottage, and she had been skittish since the lawyer next door had bled out in the park on the corner. The most sensible solution was simply for Alex and Shawna to swap – she could move into the condo, which was smaller and had a doorman, and he and Meredith could take the Kenilworth cottage. Meredith could easily sell her cheap house in Wilmette, unless she wanted to trade with Shawna, which he doubted. Everything would work out just dandy.

Alex draped his sports coat over the back of the leather sectional, grabbed the remote, and clicked on the widescreen TV. This stuff and the bed were the only furniture Alex had bought, but even the leather and chrome and the pizza boxes on the floor weren't enough to banish the ghosts of geriatric women in housecoats spritzing the wallpapered rooms with air freshener and slathering the countertops with Pinesol. He sidled into the slot kitchen and opened the freezer to prowl for something to zap for supper. He would watch the game and have a beer and try to relax for two seconds. With his heavy colonoscopy schedule on Tuesdays, he had been on his feet since six. It had been a long day.

A frozen lasagna spinning on the turntable, Alex noticed the blink of the message light on his answering machine. It was probably Shawna freaking out because the baby had sneezed, and he didn't feel like dealing with her right now. He hurried to the bedroom, where he hung his work clothes in the closet and switched to jeans and a polo shirt. Ding – that was his dinner! Time for bachelor life at its finest.

The lasagna was hot, a little black and crunchy around the edges, but if he chewed for a while, he could usually manage to get it all down. As he hunched over the counter, he tried to ignore the answering machine light, but it kept flashing in his peripheral vision and ruining what otherwise would have been a perfect moment. Rolling his eyes, he pushed the play button and blew on the cheese.

"Hi, Alex, it's Meredith. Sorry to bother you, but I thought you should know. Shawna's next door neighbor, the widow, Cece Whitaker – she died last night, killed in a hit-and-run in Winnetka. I don't know if Shawna knows, but it's been on the news. Either way – I thought you should know. Okay. Have a good night. Bye."

Shit. Shawna hadn't been at her most stable in the last few days, and this wasn't going to help. He had to admit, the body count next door was getting freakishly high, but surely there was a logical explanation. Sometimes lightening did strike twice in the same place – statistically, that happened. People came into his exam room with a bunch of symptoms that they figured were caused by the same thing, but not infrequently there were two, or even three different medical events occurring simultaneously, and fixing one was not going to solve the whole problem. Sometimes a system broke down, or maybe two things just happened by chance. But Shawna wasn't going to understand any of that. She would just figure that a serial killer was picking off residents of east Kenilworth one by one, in diabolical "accidents." She had always been a little jumpy, and now, with her hormones tanking and an infant to protect, her brain would plug into every B horror flick she had ever seen, and there were probably a lot of them.

He jammed a noodle into his mouth, chugged some water to cool his tongue, and then picked up the phone. It rang four times, and, just as the answering machine picked up and visions of eating his dinner in peace danced in his head, Shawna answered.

"Hello?" she said. Her voice sounded thin, like an overstretched wire. Behind, he could hear an infant whimper.

"Hi, it's me. Just wanted to check in." Leaning over the counter, he plunged another bite into his mouth.

"I'm not doing so well." She started to cry. Shit.

"Baby okay?" asked Alex.

"Yeah, okay. He sleeps a lot during the day. At night, not so much." In corroboration, the whimper escalated into a moderate complaint. "I'm tired."

"That's normal. Babies will be babies. Okay, then, if that's all. I'll call you tomorrow."

"That's not all. My neighbor, Cece – she was just over here, I can't believe it – she's, well, dead, she got hit by a car. Somebody killed her. And now there's a light on over there. I'm all alone, and at

81

night I'm rocking and rocking, and sometimes I hear noises. Even when Lex finally konks out, I can't sleep. What if someone comes in? I'm all alone here. Anything could happen."

"Now, now. If someone were out to get the Whitakers, they got them. And they didn't even do it in the house, they did it outside – they like the great outdoors, who can blame them? And Cece, that was in Winnetka, right? Not even your neighborhood. So I'm sure you're fine. Anyway, they were both accidents. I'm sure of it. You need a nap, that's all." Gazing toward the White Sox game on the big TV, Alex polished off the lasagna and tried to remember if he had finished the ice cream last night. He might have a Mars Bar in his briefcase.

"I don't know. I just don't feel safe. Mothers have a sixth sense about these things. I think you should come over. You can even sleep with me, we just can't, you know, do it." The baby's grousing accelerated, like a revving engine.

Alex sighed. Five days past childbirth, stitched, sticky, and half crazy, Shawna was without her usual attractions. And he was trying to prove to Meredith that he was a good man, worthy of her trust. What would she want him to do? She had called him about this, but she didn't actually tell him what she wanted. It was maddening.

"I'm kind of tired, Shawna. I don't think I'd be much good with an axe murderer." Okay, that was probably a poor line of reasoning.

"Why did you call me, then?" Shawna's pitch was rising, as if she had just inhaled helium and were about to fly into the stratosphere. Lex let out a full-throated wail.

"Well, I wanted to check on you, like I said." Okay, that was a lie. More of a fib. Still. "And Meredith called me," he said weakly. "She told me about the accident. I guess she was worried about you."

"Meredith was worried about me – hah! I am none of her business. She keeps popping up – it gives me the willies. I think she wants me dead – she wants the baby! That's it – she wants the baby, because she's too old and dried up to have one, and then I'll be out of the way, and you can all be one big happy family without me. Wouldn't life be so much simpler without me!"

Alex had to admit, she did have a point – about that last, not the rest of it. "Meredith doesn't want your baby," he said. Lex was now screaming, and Alex didn't think anyone would want him right now. "And she's too boring to kill you to get you out of her life. And if she wanted to kill you, she would have done it by now."

Shawna chortled, tinged with a touch of hysteria. "Yeah, she's boring. But I don't trust her. Once I got pregnant, the game changed."

"So now you're worried that Meredith is going to kill you. Do you hear yourself?"

"I'm not crazy. I have a sixth sense for these things. Please come over. She won't kill me if you're here."

Oh my god. The baby flitted across his brain and crossed with an image of his feet on the leather couch, his hand moving hot fudge to his face. Rats. But the baby probably shouldn't be alone at night with a psycho. "Okay, look. I'll come over. But I'm stopping at the Jewel first for some ice cream."

"Okay, fine. Could you pick up some Pampers? This kid never stops peeing." Shawna's voice was returning to a normal register.

"I will. I'll be over soon."

"Alex? Thank you."

"It's okay."

He hung up. It was tough, being a mensch. He felt like an observant Jew who thinks about the Torah while having sex. Except, although he was about to spend the night with his wife, he wasn't going to have sex. But he might give her a hug, hold her hand. And while he did, he would think about Meredith.

Chapter Eight

        Rushing from the ivy-covered church through
the hedge to the sidewalk, Clara hoped that no one
would notice her. The church was complete bullshit –
at this point, it was pretty obvious that no dude in the
sky was looking out for the good folks – but she had
to talk to somebody about her mother's funeral. Cece
had to have a funeral, everybody did, and when Dr.
Peel called, it was easy to say, yes, do what you did
for Dad. After her lame joke about a group discount,
Dr. Peel had offered to come over, but she didn't
know how to make coffee, and she didn't want him to
know she was living alone. Fake smiling when moms
delivered lasagna was bad enough, without a bunch of
church ladies trying to take over her life.
        "Clara?"
        Damn and double damn.   Her next door
neighbor had spotted her. Shawna was pushing a baby
carriage dripping with netting, like they were living in
a malarial refugee camp instead of the fanciest suburb
on the North Shore, and she looked as crappy as Clara
felt. She was wearing sweat pants the color of dried
blood with University of Chicago written down the
leg, and a stretched-out tee shirt that had been worn
for a week and barfed on a few times just this

morning. Her hair hung at weird angles, and she needed an appointment with a bra specialist. Health class ought to hire her as a spokesmodel for condom use, because nobody who went to New Trier would ever want to look like this.

"Hi," muttered Clara. If she kept walking, she might not have to fake admire the baby, who would be small and smushed, like every other baby.

"Clara, I'm so sorry. If there's anything you need...." Shawna stopped, which was annoying. If she had this kind of time, she should take a shower. And throw in a load of wash.

"Yeah," said Clara. "Thanks. Bye." She walked past, but Shawna turned the carriage around and started stalking her, which was, like, all she needed.

"Do you have enough, I don't know, food, stuff like that? I mean, I could order you a pizza."

"No thanks. I can dial a phone." Clara frowned, and Shawna looked like she was going to start sobbing right here on the sidewalk. Double shit. "I've got a lot of lasagna. Do you want some?"

"Oh, wow." She looked like she really did, but that it might look bad to take food from an orphan.

"I won't eat it. I'll leave it on your doorstep. How many do you want? I have at least six."

"One is good. Maybe two, if they're just going to get wasted. So, how are you doing? Stupid question, I'm sure."

They walked past the park. The leaves were popping open, and, through the dungeon fence, you could see the fountain, dribbling away. In the back, behind the wooden benches that nobody sat on because why would you sit there when you had cushiony ones in your giant backyard, was the lame excuse for a forest where her father had enough privacy to die. Shawna paused in front of Clara's walk, where some flowering bushes her mother had told the landscape guy to plant were blooming. Every year around this time, some guy lined their gardens with pink and white flowers. Clara wondered if he showed up automatically, like the mailman, or if she would have to do something about him.

"I should probably go now," said Clara. "Have a nice day."

"Oh, okay. Umm, do you want to see the baby? His name is Lex." Shawna lifted a blob of netting in a tantalizing way.

Clara took a polite peek. "Cute," she said.

"Listen. I've been worrying. Are you safe over there?"

"I'm an adult. I can take care of myself." Which was more than Shawna could do, from the look of her.

"Okay, sure. It's just – I can't help but notice, you've had kind of a run of bad luck."

Clara looked at the park. "That's true," she said. "So what?"

"Well, I don't know. Silly, I guess." Shawna started to sniff. "I'm just worried."

Whoa, this was way weird. Clara was the one whose mother had just died, and this lady was losing it. The baby started to fuss. It was a strange thought, but maybe Shawna needed help more than Clara did.

"You know," said Clara, "I could watch him for a minute – if you want to wash or something. I mean, just on the chance. If you don't mind that I don't know anything about babies."

"Really?" Shawna wiped her eyes. "That would be wonderful. I haven't had a shower in a couple days."

"I couldn't tell," said Clara.

Shawna laughed a little. "Yeah. And you can't be any worse at taking care of him than I am."

"That's not true. I mean, I'm sure you do fine." Okay, whatever, maybe this would be a nice distraction. Everybody said that doing good deeds made you feel better, though Clara had never actually tried it. There was also something about no good deed going unpunished. People could never make up their minds, just like about eating carbs and real butter – good or bad? At least Shawna looked a little perked up. "Just hang on a sec, and I'll get the lasagna."

"Thanks so much. Do you want to stay for lunch? We could have lasagna." Shawna actually smiled.

"Umm, okay," said Clara. "My house feels, I don't know. Weird," she admitted.

"Weird how?" Shawna's eyes widened.

"I don't know. I keep thinking I hear my mother walking around." Clara was actually a little concerned about this. She had even heard her mother calling her from downstairs this morning, which was psycho.

"You've had a huge loss. You're traumatized. It'll go away after a while." Shawna pushed back a hunk of her hair. "I'm a little crazy myself right now."

"I thought this was supposed to be the happiest day of your life, or something." said Clara.

"Yeah, right," said Shawna. "I'll tell you a secret. It's all a big scam."

"Life's a scam," said Clara. "Nothing turns out like it should." She scraped the toe of her sandal against the sidewalk.

"Yeah," said Shawna. "I don't know if I should tell you this, but what the hell. My marriage is breaking up. He wants to go back to his ex-wife."

"Whoa," said Clara. This lady had a more interesting life than she thought. "That's nuts. Why did he leave her in the first place, then?"

"Good question. He seems to have forgotten about that. Men are idiots. Sorry. We should be talking about you."

"No. It's good," said Clara. "I mean...."

"Glad my misery can be of service. Go get the lasagna."

"Okay," said Clara. "Thanks."

"Thank you," said Shawna.

Opening the back door, Meredith transitioned from the D.U.I. in her head to a domestic kitchen scene. Maggie stood at the sink peeling carrots over the garbage disposal, while Lucy manned a wooden spoon, stirring a saucepan on the stove. The room smelled like her childhood – baked chicken, sugar, and Jergens lotion. Meredith's mother, in a dining room chair pulled center stage, provided supervision. Smiling, Meredith circled the counter to peck the cheeks of her favorite females.

"I'm teaching Lucy to make mashed potatoes," said Sara. "I can't believe she doesn't know how. You made them every week at her age."

Instant potato flakes dotted the stovetop like snow. Although she had happily consumed large quantities of this convenience food as a child, Meredith snobbishly refused to cook them as an adult. As a result, they never ate mashed potatoes at all.

"Where did you get those, Mom? Did you go shopping?" Meredith moved next to Maggie to wash her hands.

"Of course not," said Sara. "I brought them in my suitcase. There was a very good sale at Albertson's, buy one, get one free. I brought you the free one."

"Lucy made Grandma's yellow cake mix," said Maggie. "And I made the frosting from scratch."

"They did a wonderful job," said Sara.

With the heat of cooking, the company of her granddaughters, and a few dabs from an ancient pot of rouge, Sara's complexion had pinked-up encouragingly. "How are you feeling, Mom?"

"I'm doing very well, thank you. We accomplished a great deal today. We straightened up and vacuumed, and we even did a load of wash. Very productive. And no TV."

"Except 'Jeopardy,'" said Maggie. "It's educational."

"Exactly," said Sara.

"I had to dust the whole house. Grandma just sat around." Lucy twirled a strand of hair and knocked the spoon against the sides of the pot in an aggrieved manner.

"Turn that off now, Lucy," said Sara. "Someone has to supervise, or no one will work, and the house will burn down."

"But tomorrow, I'm going to the beach," said Maggie. "Right, Mom?"

"That's fine," said Sara. "The house is clean, and we made double chicken, and there's plenty of cake. You're taking your sister?"

"I'm sure Lucy can make her own plans," Meredith interjected, as Maggie's jaw dropped open. "I'm going to go upstairs to change, and then, dinner!"

"She just walks in here and eats our food," said Lucy.

"Your mother made the money to buy this food," said Sara.

"Not the potatoes," said Lucy, "or the cake."

Meredith went into her bedroom and shut the door. While having her mother here could make everyone feel like a kindergartener, Sara did seem to be recovering her health. In fact, despite predictable griping from the adolescent crowd, the three of them seemed to be thriving. Meredith kicked off her work shoes, stripped off her pantsuit, and pulled on a short-sleeved blouse and a pair of jeans. In the bathroom, she washed her face and poofed her curly hair. Sara might appreciate a dab of lipstick, but Meredith would just eat it off. She drew the line on people-pleasing at the needless consumption of carcinogens.

Back downstairs, Meredith found her family propped around the dining room table before plates of the same sort of uninspiring but nutritious food that Meredith cooked herself, with the added flourish that the barbecue sauce appeared in a bowl with a teaspoon. They all looked pleased with themselves, though a little irritated with everyone else.

"Thank you," Meredith said, nodding around the table. "This looks delicious."

"You're welcome," said Sara.

"We did it all," said Lucy.

"Shut up," said Maggie.

Sara looked down at her plate. At first, Meredith thought that, from fatigue and these last contentious moments with her ungrateful grandchildren, her mother was trying not to cry. On closer inspection, Meredith realized that what she had taken as a quivering lip was actually Sara whispering to herself.

"Are you okay, Mom?" asked Meredith. "You know, if you girls can't get along, you're going to have to be excused. Which would be a shame, because this dinner looks terrific."

"I'm fine, I'm wonderful," said Sara, picking up her fork. "Just saying a little thank you, for all of my blessings. And I should say it to all of you. Thank you for letting me stay here, for being so kind and generous. You are my family, and I love you very much. It's wonderful to be together."

"We love you too," said Meredith, "and we're happy that you're here. So," she continued, "A change of subject. I was thinking of coming home early tomorrow, to take you girls to see your new brother."

"Seen him," said Maggie. "No thanks. I'm going to the beach, remember?"

"Yeah, no thanks," said Lucy. "Anyway, he's only my half brother."

"What does that mean?" asked Meredith.

"It means that half of me thinks he's a dumb baby who cries all the time, and the other half thinks he's got nothing to do with me. I've got enough problems without him," said Lucy.

Taking a sip of ice water, Meredith looked at her children with some surprise. They hadn't been exposed to babies much, but she thought that most kids – most girls, she had to admit – liked babies. And Lex was just a baby. As hard as it was for Meredith to see him and block out nauseating images of the intimacy that had produced him, none of this was his fault. He had two older sisters, and they ought to be a family somehow.

"Well, I'm still going to stop by Shawna's house. I think she could use some help, and I think you two should come. The baby's cute, right Maggie?"

"Adorable. May I please be excused?"

It was amazing how quickly her children could hoover up a plate of food. Meredith wondered if a day would ever arrive when either of them would ask her a real question at dinner. If Maggie had said, "Well, Mom, what did you do today?" Meredith would have dropped down dead. Meanwhile, Sara was nibbling mashed potato and moving chicken around on her plate.

"Wait just a minute. I want you two to come with me. Lex," Meredith choked out the name, "is your brother."

"Why?" asked Maggie. "Because he's Dad's? I haven't seen Dad living around here lately. Maybe if Dad ever decides we're his daughters, maybe then we can decide that baby is our brother. But I'm sorry, Mom, no offense, but I just don't see it happening." Maggie stood, tossed her figure around, and flounced out of the room.

"Clear your place, please," called Meredith.

"I'll do it," said Lucy. She picked up her plate and Maggie's, carried them to the kitchen, and followed her sister upstairs.

"They left their glasses," said Sara.

"They always do."

Sara opened her mouth to call them, and then changed her mind. "Well, this will give us some time to talk." Leaning back in her chair, she smoothed the front of her cardigan, buttoned over a long-sleeved blouse and a pullover sweater. The line on her bifocals dividing her eyes somewhat mitigated their concerned expression. "Meredith, you're a wonderful mother," said Sara. "But in some ways you're too easy on them, and in some ways too hard."

"I get tired of telling them what to do," said Meredith.

"I know," said Sara. "But, what about this baby business?"

"Is that me being too easy or too hard?" Suddenly, Meredith felt very tired.

"You think you should be going over to that house. Helping out. Bonding with the baby. Lucy says she has enough problems right now. Don't you?"

"I don't know. I mean, you've been sick, that worries me. And the girls are home for the summer, and with me working, that's always a bit of anxiety. But they're pretty big now."

"Yes. But that's not what I mean. Alex just runs through here like he owns the place, and you seem fine with that."

"He's Maggie and Lucy's father."

"That's as may be. He is also married to a young woman who just had his baby. What do you

94

think is going to happen? Do you think he's going to come back to you."

"I don't know, Mom. He says he wants to come back. The good part of me wants him to, I don't know – to love me, and to take care of everyone. He has responsibilities to that baby, and if he ignores them, what would that say about him?"

"So you're trying to do what, exactly – create a polygamous family with three children and two wives? Is that what you really want?"

Meredith started to cry. "What I want doesn't matter. I'll never get what I want. What I want is to erase the last five years, to have a do-over, where Alex is happy and I'm happy and he stays in the nice, simple family that we had, that I thought we had. But I can't have what I want. So I'm trying to do what's right."

"It wasn't your fault, Meredith. It was Alex's fault and Shawna's. He's the one who has to make it right. He hurt you. He's still hurting you." Sara reached her hand out toward Meredith and rested it on the table. Meredith could see the veins and tendons, like twigs under her thin, splotchy skin.

"He can't help it, Mom. There's a baby. That was a bad call – you're right, that hurts. But the baby is a human being, and yes, a part of this family."

"But you don't have to rub your face in it."

"It's awful, I know it's awful. But I don't know what to do. I'm trying to do the right thing," Meredith repeated. She picked up her fork and started smashing stray carrots into blobs of mashed potato.

"I think you're trying to make it easier for Alex. But this isn't easy. Do you think Shawna's going to make it easy? She can't like you very much right now. Because of you – not your fault...."

"I know. My animal magnetism." Meredith stabbed some chicken fat and then dropped her fork back on her plate.

"Well, because Alex is such a mess, Shawna is all alone with that new baby. She must be going crazy -- crazy enough to want him back. You know she's not going to let him go, she named the child after him. Do you think she wants a nice big happy family with all of us here? She wants her baby and her husband. If I had to guess, I would say she is plotting right now to get Alex back, and to get you and Maggie and Lucy completely out of the picture."

"You give her too much credit, Mom. She isn't that clever. And she loves Maggie and Lucy."

"Maybe," said Sara. "Or maybe she loved them before she had her own baby, and he changes everything."

Sara started to cough. Meredith stood up and rubbed her mother's back. "We should get those girls down here to help with the dishes," Sara choked.

"Mom, I want you to go upstairs and rest. You've done a lot today, it's enough. Thank you for dinner. And I like to do the dishes by myself. Honestly."

"Alright, well. But those girls need to learn to help out."

"I know. Go on up."

Meredith picked up her plate and Sara's, and then she watched her mother grab the railing and make her slow, stooped way up the stairs, step by deliberate step. Sara had lived a long time, she had the benefit of experience. But she didn't know

96

everything, and the fact that she was sure of herself didn't make her right. Meredith had to remember that her mother was an old-fashioned woman burdened with a lot of stereotypes about how people should live. Sara was going to have to realize that, sometimes, Meredith knew best.

Chapter Nine

Ellen had to hand it to Cece, even in death she knew how to attract an audience. The entire village of Kenilworth must have followed the bloody breadcrumbs from their breakfast table *Tribunes* to the church door. Men in dark suits with stern expressions and women in narrow skirts and matching peplum jackets crammed the pews and overwhelmed the stench of the many floral tributes with their expensive aftershaves and colognes. An usher handed Ellen a program sporting a photo of Cece in full gala regalia, diamond earrings dangling below a stiff blonde updo, her blue eyes bright with several cocktails. Walking the red carpet, Ellen noted the walnut casket, dripping with lilies, slammed tight in the front of the church. Ah, the beauteous Cece, lovely no more – not even North Shore morticians could rehabilitate her to a state suitable for viewing by genteel company. And what would happen to those diamond earrings now? Ellen hoped that Clara wasn't fool enough to have chucked them into the coffin with the grisly remains.

Picking her way down the aisle toward the rustic cross hanging above the casket like a medieval threat, Ellen wondered why Cece had attended this church, instead of the grander nouveau gothic one across the street. This small sanctuary, with its wood-beamed ceiling and stiff pews, looked more like the rural church where Robin Hood would have conspired with Friar Tuck than the spiritual home of a congregation with an average family income ten times the poverty line. Perhaps the dim lighting flattered her aging complexion. Certainly Sanford wouldn't have cared, unless filling shoe boxes with hotel toiletries for the poor forwarded his law firm's networking agenda. Ellen checked her watch – it was 1:15, and she had missed lunch and a conference call to drive back from downtown to attend this event. She hoped she wouldn't have to trek to the cemetery too. If Clara had any sense, which was doubtful considering her age and maternal genome, she would feed the whole mess into the furnace and save the rest of the family a boatload of bullshit. Why Ellen should grieve a woman who never gave her a moment's consideration, she honestly could not fathom.

From behind, Ellen spotted two streaky blonde heads perched side-by-side on the front row, one clearly Clara, and the other, some freakish interloper. Turning the corner, she saw Clara, dripping black in a caricature of funeral garb, quivering beside a thirtyish woman who, from the look of her paunch and her general hygiene, had just given birth to the fetus in a sailor suit sprawled across her lap. At first eye contact, Clara coiled to stand and scream at Ellen, something inappropriate and blood-curdling that would have Kenilworth talking for weeks. But, in an exhibit of self-control that would have made her mother proud, she looked at the floor and whimpered.

"Hello, Clara. So sorry for your loss," said Ellen. "I believe this is my seat," she said, turning to Clara's clone of Christmas future. "This row is reserved for family."

"This is my next-door neighbor, Shawna Bennett," said Clara. "And you are not my family."

"Sorry," said Shawna. "I was just saying hello, and the baby is heavy."

"This happens all the time at work," said Ellen. "Women use their children as an excuse to make everyone else's life more difficult. You'll have to excuse me for not making your baby my top priority today." Shawna gathered herself and hurried to the back of the sanctuary. "You're welcome," said Ellen, turning back to Clara, "for saving you from a wailing baby during the service. That child shouldn't be here. People are so thoughtless."

"You're a monster," said Clara. "Get away from me."

"Hello, Clara." Alan wheeled up dragging Jessica, in one of her many heinous smock dresses.

Ellen thrust out her hand. "Jessica! Such a chipper outfit on this terrible day. Daddy would be pleased."

"What?"

Alan eased his arm around Jessica's shoulders. "We're here to support Clara. How are you, Clara?"

"How do you think I am? You should all go back to work. I'm sure that's where you want to be."

"Nonsense," said Ellen. "We're delighted to be here. Oh, look, here comes my husband."

100

"Clara," said Mason. "So sorry for your loss. Please, if there's anything I can do…."

"Not now, Mason," said Alan.

Jessica knelt in front of Clara, a technique she had undoubtedly perfected reassuring three-year-olds. "I know this is very difficult. But your mother will be back."

"What are you talking about?" Clara met her gaze in genuine perplexity.

"Well, I mean, you'll see her again. In heaven, right? I mean, she's not really dead, right?"

"Oh my God," said Clara.

"Shhh, it's about to start," said Ellen, plopping down next to Clara. Alan sat on Clara's right, leaving the spouses at the ends of the pew.

In a white robe with a black sash, Dr. Peel stood before Clara like the angel of death. Raising his arms, he tried to quiet the murmurs about the juicy hit-and-run – so shocking, such a shame, and the shooting, poor family, when everyone was really trying to figure out what her parents had done to bring this on themselves. What was Cece thinking, walking in the ravines after dark, so unsafe, they would never do anything that irresponsible, and with her daughter along, bad mothering too. And how many drinks had she consumed? And the father – well – honestly, who brings a gun to the park, there must have been some problem, money or drugs, of course the whole house imploded after that unsavory fiasco. Too bad about the daughter, well, she seemed sweet enough, but she didn't stand a chance applying to the Ivies, despite that desperate Hail Mary with the badminton team. Though, with two parents dead, she might have an edge on the application essay. And then they would get worried and start to pick at their manicures.

Everything seemed to be happening in a different dimension, and all by itself. Yesterday a church lady had come over and asked for an outfit for Cece to wear, and Clara had given her Cece's favorite pajamas, the plaid flannel ones she saved for when Sanford was out of town, so that she would be comfy for all eternity. But the lady said no, it wasn't appropriate, Cece wouldn't like it, she would want to look her best. Then Clara had cried, because she couldn't imagine her mother would ever look her best again, and the lady tiptoed upstairs and pulled out a black cocktail dress and the Christian Louboutin's that pinched. Clara didn't know whether to hope that the shoes were on her mother's feet or in the lady's closet, where they couldn't hurt Cece anymore. Later the funeral home called, and she told them to do whatever, it didn't matter now.

Somehow, a coffin had appeared at Clara's feet, with a bunch of smelly flowers on top, and, she supposed, her mother inside. Dr. Peel was gesturing, and his mouth was moving, but she couldn't focus. Then the organ played, something churchy, and the choir was up there now, white people in white robes singing something about a deer and cooling streams. Clara thought they shot deer in Winnetka, or maybe they only gave them birth control, but her mother had said there was some gigantic problem, because deer were coming in people's yards and eating their shrubbery. A cooling stream sounded nice in theory, but it was actually kind of cold in the church, a sort of natural air-conditioning, like a tomb or a cave. Clara wondered if Cece would be cold in the ground, and she hoped that the lady had wrapped her in a blanket, and she knew that she hadn't, because that wouldn't be appropriate, and she almost stood up. But Alan must have noticed, because he grabbed her arm with the hand that wasn't holding Jessica's, and he asked her if she wanted to breathe into a paper bag, because Mason had stopped at Dunkin' Donuts, and Clara gagged a little. Then Alan switched seats with Jessica, who put her arm around Clara in a shaky way, which actually felt good.

Dr. Peel said, "Christ has been raised from the dead, the first fruits of those who have died." He kept going for a long time, while Clara thought about fruit. Fruit was something your mother fed you when you were just a baby, the squashed kind in jars, like pears or applesauce. Fruit was better than vegetables, which mothers tried to get their kids to eat, but they wouldn't. What did it mean for Jesus to be a fruit – what kind of fruit would he be? Maybe he had to be a date or a fig, in his desert location, though God could do anything he wanted. And if God could do anything He wanted, why was her mother dead? Why were they in this church acting like He was some sort of good guy? Clara started to stand up again, but this time Ellen pinched her, and she started to cry. Jessica rubbed her back and said that everything would be okay. But if that was because her mother was alive, then that was another lie. When Dr. Peel said they could all go to the social hall for lemonade and brownies, Clara and Jessica went out the side door into the churchyard, and in front of the beautiful wall of ivy-draped memorial stones, they both threw up. It was nice to have company for that.

After the usual Friday workload of speeders, and despite her mother's advice to back off, Meredith decided to check on Shawna before knocking back a large glass of chardonnay at home to toast the weekend. Despite having lived in Kenilworth before her divorce, Meredith was now used to her own Wilmette block, family houses packed tight enough to elicit hellos and a little friendly chatter when neighbors shoveled their walks or watered their lawns. Shutting the car door, she marveled at Shawna's neighborhood. Here, no one watered his own grass, unless punching on the underground sprinkler system counted, and yards were huge, though houses were still close enough for residents to glimpse someone inside at night if the shades weren't drawn. Winding up Shawna's walkway, Meredith admired the hydrangeas, persistently blooming despite a fringe of brown leaves that the customary spring clean-up should have blasted into a truck heading for a dump in a cheaper town. Clearly, Alex had failed to re-up the yard guy. Hopefully this casual attitude toward plants did not extend to the helpless animal she now heard keening inside the house.

Meredith rang the doorbell and waited. She was tired from a week's work and would have loved to go home, wash her face, and eat the kung pao chicken that she planned to pick up on her way back. But she hadn't seen Shawna since Sunday, and, what with the new baby and the dead neighbor, she felt she should check in. Either that, or this was a train wreck that she couldn't stop ogling, a sore that she had to scratch until it bled. Because Shawna was not her friend, and seeing Alex's son made her ill. But this was a new mother, with whom she had more than a passing acquaintance, living alone with her newborn - - shouldn't she drop by now and then to offer some support? And how much more so, when the baby was Maggie and Lucy's brother – and, if she and Alex reconciled, her own stepson? This was a difficult situation, but one that needed to be faced.

Meredith rang the bell again, chimes punctuating the baby's wails. After another pause and a series of knocks, she turned the doorknob and shoved. When the door opened, the bungie cord between her chest and any anxious baby yanked her into the living room, which looked like the aftermath of a Babies R Us explosion. Hopping among diapers, wipes, small blankets, and half-drunk cups of what she hoped was mushroom soup, Meredith followed the cries past the bassinet to the far corner of the room, where tiny Lex drooped in the well of a bucket car seat. A stream of spit-up spun from his mouth to everything in his vicinity – the seat cover, his blanket, his surprising sailor suit, and somehow, the living room rug. His face glowed red, his fists thrashed. He was furious.

Scanning the floor for a cleanish cloth, Meredith grabbed a towel, pulled it over her shoulder, and eased Lex into her arms. Despite his sour upper reek, yeasty bottom smell, and distressing Alex-plus-Shawna provenance, she wanted him close against her, comforted and secure. Although it had been almost twelve years since Lucy's birth, the motor memory prompted her to rub his back and bounce. As she peeled him forward to dab his face, Shawna rushed downstairs.

"What the hell do you think you're doing?" Damp hair framed her flushed cheeks, and her vaguely tied robe gaped open to reveal a massive volume of breast tissue.

"No one answered the door. I'm just trying to calm him down."

"Give him to me!" Snatching her baby, Shawna jerked his head, and his face pinched for a scream. She dropped into a chair and jammed a nipple in his mouth. Immediately, he quieted. "I was taking a bath. Is that a crime?"

"Of course not," said Meredith, lowering herself onto the sofa between a stuffed bear and a onesie. "But as soon as you hit the water, the baby wakes up. It's a law of nature."

"That still doesn't give you the right to barge in here."

"No. I'm sorry. I just wanted to see how you're doing, especially after – next door." Shawna didn't say anything. Lex turned his face away and sighed. "Do you want to eat something? I can hold him. Give you a break."

"I would like to get some clothes on." Shawna eyed Meredith warily.

"Sure. I could come upstairs and change him, if that's okay."

Shawna stood up. "Alright, if you leave the nursery door open. But no funny business."

Meredith followed Shawna upstairs. She wasn't sure what Shawna was worried about, but she had nothing funny in mind, so she decided to go with it. Shawna settled Lex, now in a trance, on the changing table. Rummaging through organic bottom creams, Meredith could hear Shawna slamming around in what was formerly the Alex-plus-Shawna marital bedroom. Meredith was not going anywhere near that room. She did not want to see the bed, she did not want to imagine pre-baby Shawna sliding between the sheets in a slinky negligee, or worse, her slinky skin, and Alex reaching over to touch her, to love her. What on earth was she doing, changing Lex's diaper, a child who had come from their love, or at least, from their sex? No, she refused to think about that. Meredith wiped his bottom clean and pressed a diaper between his legs. Then she felt among the shelves for a clean terry jumpsuit.

Coming up empty, she lugged Lex to the bunny-stenciled dresser, which contained sunhats, booties, and an assortment of christening gowns and size 2T overalls. Waiting for Shawna's advice, she picked up the stuffed rabbit on top of the dresser, next to the shadow lamp. Behind it, at the edge of the lace runner, was one of the largest butcher knives that Meredith had seen outside Benihana of Tokyo. Horrified, she placed Lex in his bassinet, where he began to complain. She picked up the knife, and Shawna rushed in.

"What the hell are you doing?" she screamed. "Stay away from my baby!"

Meredith set the knife at the end of the dresser farthest from Shawna and put up her hands. "What the hell is that knife doing up here?"

Shawna turned pale. She leaped past Meredith and pulled Lex, now pink and flustered, into her arms.

"I want you out of here, you witch! Get out of my house, before I call the police!"

Meredith didn't know what to do. She wanted to get the knife out of the room, or better, out of the house. Even if there were a perfectly reasonable, though hard to imagine, explanation for its appearance in the nursery, she did not want to leave a giant sharp weapon in plain sight with a sleep-deprived mother and an apoplectic infant. On the other hand, Shawna was bound to take Meredith's grabbing the knife and walking in her direction poorly. It was her knife and her house, and Shawna had every right to kick Meredith out and keep her legal kitchen-aid/instrument-of-doom anywhere she pleased. As Shawna shielded the baby, Meredith moved the stuffed bunny back to hide the knife and slid past Shawna and down the stairs.

"I couldn't find his clean clothes," Meredith called. "But I changed his diaper."

Shawna moved to the top of the stairs. "And don't ever come back," she shouted.

Meredith didn't reply. She opened the front door and closed it behind her with a click. Beside her car, she paused for a moment to breathe. The evening was lovely, warm and fragrant, and pansies bloomed in pots and gardens all over the block. In a couple of weeks, yardmen would yank them out, toss them in garbage bins, and replace them with impatiens and geraniums. Sometimes one thing had to be pulled out and thrown in the trash for the next thing to grow and thrive. Maybe her mother was right. Pansies and impatiens just did not live together in one happy garden. But how could she turn her back on Alex's baby? The knife flashed through her mind again, its glinting edge, its ability to ruin lives forever in one terrible second. Maybe she should call Alex. But no, what was she trying to do, push Alex and Shawna together again? But the knife. Meredith got into her car, pulled out her cell phone and punched in his number. As much as she wished that Lex had never been born, as much as she wished that he would vanish in a magical puff of smoke, she just couldn't take a chance.

Chapter Ten

Alex rang the bell twice. He loved those chimes, just like jolly old England, where he planned to go with Meredith once everything settled down and they moved in here together. He imagined sleeping on the plane to minimize his time away from work, snuggled together in business class like two little bears in La-Z-Boys. He knocked and turned the doorknob, just as Shawna turned it from the inside.

Alex had forgotten how attractive Shawna could look if she stopped being pregnant and put on deodorant. He could feel heat coming off her skin, and the dark roots at the base of her hair were sexy in a jungle sort of way. Her eyes looked smoky with sleep deprivation, and, trying to focus, she blinked them in a way he would describe as coy, with a hint of cayenne pepper. And then, below -- the jeans snug, and the blouse straining. Mesmerized by the tug on her center button, Alex plunged his hand in his pants pocket and shifted uncomfortably. Seduction had always been her strength.

"Come in," Shawna said, opening the door wide. "You look good."

"Thanks. So do you." Shawna appeared decidedly less crazy than she had four days ago, when he last saw her. Yesterday Meredith had wanted him to check on her, but Meredith could be a bit mothery. The business about the butcher knife in the baby's room was strange, but Alex's father had carried a Swiss Army knife in his pocket for years. It didn't mean he wanted to murder anyone -- he just wanted to open beer bottles and heavily taped packages without having to rummage around. Shawna must have brought the knife upstairs to open a baby gift and then forgotten it.

Stepping around a laundry basket full of onesies, he couldn't help but spot a nursing bra, its cup unlatched and lolling open. Alex wondered if Shawna were wearing one now, and he shifted again. She touched his arm, and he jumped.

"The babysitter should be here in a minute. Do you want to see your son?"

"Sure," he said. Alex followed her up the stairs, her buttocks ticking like a pocket watch. He tried to forget the times he had grabbed her, friskily when they first got married, and later, more savagely, after fights about his work hours and his relationship with Meredith. In the nursery, a shadow lamp threw silhouettes around the walls in an eerie dance, and he heard a rhythmic murmur, like an asthmatic ogre curled up under the floorboards.

"What's that noise?" he asked, tiptoeing toward the crib.

"It's ocean sounds. From the sheep." Shawna motioned toward a dismembered head dangling from the crib slats. Peering, Alex saw his son. He was beautiful.

"Hi Lex," he said softly.

"Of course he's sleeping now, with a babysitter coming. But that's okay, he let me get dressed. He must want his parents to have a nice time."

"Hello?" a voice called tentatively from the front hall.

"Up here!" said Shawna. "That's Clara, she lives next door. Her mother just died in a car accident. Clara got hurt too, but she's fine. She offered to babysit."

As Alex opened his mouth, Clara entered the room. In the shadowy light, she looked gray, like a princess turned to stone. "Hello, Clara," he said, bowing slightly. "Are you sure you're up to this? I'm sorry for your loss."

"It's fine, it's good," she said. Her eyes stared, words emerging from her mouth by rote. "It's good for me to get out of the house."

"Okay, well, you know best," said Shawna. "Lex is sleeping in here. If he wakes up, you can give him one of these bottles. They gave them to me at the hospital, they're all set. I turned on the baby monitor in the family room, so you can watch TV down there. Just make yourself at home. Thanks! See ya! Bye!"

She hurried toward the stairs. Alex turned to Clara. "I guess we're going," he said.

"That's fine."

"I'll call you in a little while, just to make sure everything's going okay. We won't be long, just a quick dinner."

"She has my cell phone number," called Shawna.

"Have fun," said Clara. "Don't worry. We'll be fine."

Alex stopped and touched her hand. It was cold. "Are you sure about this? You've been through a lot."

"I have been through a lot, but that will protect me," said Clara. "I mean, what else could possibly go wrong?"

Clara watched Shawna ease herself into the passenger seat of Alex's Mercedes – nice car, if a bit old man, but Alex still scored amphibian in the *Glamour* survey, "Your Guy: Prince or Frog," considering he bailed when Shawna was pregnant. He had been attentive to Clara, which was sweet in a way, but also kind of gross. From what Shawna said, Alex was confused, which just made him an idiot. He had a hot wife and a new baby – why blow that for some middle-aged yawn he had already dumped once? If Sanford had ever considered going back to April and their freaky children, Cece would have had him committed.

Clara wandered downstairs and into the kitchen. She was tired, she hadn't been sleeping, and she might not have eaten for a while. If you had asked Clara her mother's top characteristic two weeks ago, she would have said that Cece was annoying, with her snoopy questions about Clara's day and her pushy attempts to run her life. But now, hearing her mother tell her to put on a sweater and stay out of the chips would have been a dream come true.

Apparently she didn't have to worry about money, which hadn't even occurred to her until one of her father's law partners pulled her aside after Cece's funeral to tell her she was rich. Since her mother died without a will, all of Cece's property, the money, the house, everything she had inherited from Sanford, would go to Clara, her only child. Clara would own the whole house, most of what was in it, and most of her father's money. Which was a huge relief, if she actually thought about it.

Still, she couldn't sleep. Sometimes she heard murmurs, like her parents talking in the next room, but every time she checked, just to be sure, no one was there. She was alone, she was always alone. Clara opened Shawna's fridge to see if she had any nonfat yogurt or a salad-in-a-bag. If she could choke down a few lettuce leaves, that would probably pep her up, but when she took one bite of anything, her stomach just sealed up.

Shawna definitely needed to make a grocery run, but she did have bread, and a toaster you needed a PhD in engineering to operate. Clara took a slice of white bread out of its plastic bag, dropped it in a toaster slot, and fiddled around until she finally found a button that lowered the bread between two heating coils. Kind of a disturbing process, if you were the bread. The world was a pretty ghastly place, all in all.

Clara didn't know where the plates were, but she found a paper towel, and when the toast popped up, she used it to carry her meal into the family room. Everything was quiet, except for a rustling from the baby monitor that actually was kind of soothing -- like a mom's heart beat or stomach gurgles -- sounds a baby might hear when she was safe inside a uterus, just chilling and growing, floating around, but attached to her mom by a life line. It would be awesome to be back inside her mother, with no worries, everything calm and secure. But then she would be swimming in her mother's guts, which was totally disgusting, and eventually she would have to get squeezed out her vagina. And besides, her mother was dead. If she were inside her mother now, she would be dead too. Clara sat on the couch and set her toast on a magazine. She put her head between her knees, just to rest for a moment. It might feel good to pass out, but she was supposed to be babysitting.

Sitting up, she found the remote control under a dish towel. A little trashy TV might take her mind off things. Settling back against the couch, she kicked off her sandals and rested her feet on the coffee table between a glass of watery Coke and a bowl of Dorito crumbs. Normally she would be out with friends on Saturday night, but no one wanted to hang out with her. They wanted to have fun, not sit around moping in front of "Dr. Quinn, Medicine Woman," which seemed to be her only option tonight. A couple friends did call to ask her how she was doing, but if she told them how miserable and scared and nuts she felt, they wouldn't know what to say. So, she told them she was keeping busy, which was true, because here she was, holding down a responsible job.

Closing her eyes, Clara could hear Dr. Quinn muttering in the background, something about a dangerous infection that she could treat with herbs from the forest. Clara was so tired, and the voice was soothing. Once they found these herbs everything would be okay, no one would die, everything was fixable with Dr. Quinn in charge. After a few minutes, she heard crying, like Dr. Quinn had a new patient, and then she heard a door open and close. Some new mother, possibly a Native American, must have brought her baby to Dr. Quinn's examining room, if she had one, Clara had never actually seen the show before. She probably worked from a special home office, because that definitely sounded more like the door to a house on the prairie, not to some wigwam, which would just have a flap, or some half-buried sod house, which would be hard to locate in the Wild West when you were sick and needed the doctor's help. As Clara dozed, the baby's cries became louder, drowning out the TV characters until finally, she realized that no professional TV director would let a baby just scream his head off, and maybe the baby was the real one that she was supposed to be listening for. Her eyes sprang open, and she sat up straight, and just as she was preparing to leap off the couch and turn around to head upstairs, to do god knows what to comfort Lex, she heard a very loud noise, like a car back-firing, and then, almost on top of it, another noise just like it, and she fell sideways onto the peach couch. As her blood soaked into the cushions and dripped onto the custom-made floral rug and mixed with some cookie crumbs, she saw her mother floating over her head, telling her that it was all over now. They would be together in heaven, where there were no creepy relatives or badminton practice or loneliness. So that, when she died, what she finally felt was relief.

"I told you we should have skipped dessert," Alex said, rushing up the front walk.

"I know, but that chocolate cake looked delicious, and I never get to go anywhere." It was a lovely evening, the sky velvety gray with a zillion watts of Chicago electricity and the glow of Kenilworth's old-fashioned street lamps. "Clara was probably in the bathroom when you called." So, Lex was fussing – he was obviously fine, just mad. "He always gets his way. It won't hurt him to have to wait a minute." As Alex rummaged in his pocket for the house key, Shawna reached out and opened the door.

"Didn't you lock up?"

"So what?"

Shawna followed Alex upstairs, where Lex was stroking out. His face was red, his mouth pinched, and everything was wet – his cheeks, his suit, and the crib sheet, where a pool of spit-up soured on both sides of his head. Now that Shawna had devoured a steak and a salad and a chunk of cake garnished with two glasses of wine and some heavy flirting, Lex had shrunk from the ravenous gullet of her nightmares to the pathetic little bundle that he really was. Lifting him with a clean receiving blanket, she settled into the rocking chair and tugged up her blouse.

"I'll go see what happened to Clara," Alex said. "She'd better still be here."

"Don't you want to stay and watch me?" Shawna asked, but Alex was distracted. "She probably tried everything and gave up. Lex can get pretty exasperating. I wouldn't blame her."

"Maybe you shouldn't have hired her the day after her mother's funeral."

"Listen to yourself, you are so judgy. Anyway, I don't care. Everyone survived, and I so needed the night out. Lex is fine. It was totally worth it."

Alex tromped down the stairs, while Lex snorted, smothering in breast tissue. After a few minutes, Alex returned. He looked pale.

"Okay," he said. "I called 911. They want us to go outside. Right now."

Shawna heard a siren, and then another one. With Lex still latched to her breast, she stood up. "What's wrong? Is there a fire?"

"Just come outside."

Alex put his arm around Shawna, and they walked downstairs and out the front door. Two police cars came, and a fire truck, and an ambulance. Neighbors she had never met emerged from their front doors to stare. Defiantly, Shawna switched Lex to the other side, her used breast drooping damply under her blouse, as two policemen walked toward them.

"I'm Officer Dart, hello," said the taller, cuter one. Both cops nodded and turned to Alex. "Are you Dr. Bennett?"

Two paramedics hurried up behind them. "Yes, Dr. Alexander Bennett, and this is my – wife, Shawna. She's in the family room."

"No, I'm not. I'm right here," said Shawna.

"We'll check the house and the perimeter," said Officer Dart, pulling a flashlight from his belt.

"What's going on?" asked Shawna.

"We need to make sure the perpetrator has vacated the scene," said Officer Dart.

"Our babysitter, Clara, she must be in there." Shawna's stomach turned, and she looked at Alex. "I think I have to sit down," she said.

"Here." Alex led Shawna to his Mercedes, now surrounded by emergency vehicles.

"Don't go anywhere, we'll want to talk to both of you," called Officer Dart, as he shined his flashlight into the hydrangeas.

Alex opened the car door and waited while Shawna, with Lex now sleeping in her arms, slid across the backseat. He followed and slammed the door, as neighbors inched closer, and the paramedics returned to the ambulance. "What's going on?" asked Shawna. "Did something happen to Clara?"

Alex took her hand. "She's in the family room. She may have been – shot. I think she's dead."

"Oh my god," said Shawna, as the paramedics wheeled a stretcher up the walk.

Officer Dart knocked on the car door, and Alex opened it. "We're checking the house now, to make sure there is no intruder still on the premises. You know the victim?"

"Yes, it's Clara – what is it, Whitaker?" Alex turned to Shawna, who nodded.

"She lives next door," said Shawna. "She was babysitting. We just went out to dinner. Oh my god, Lex could have been killed."

"She appears to be the same Clara Whitaker whose mother was killed in a hit-and-run earlier this week," said Officer Dart. "Was she depressed?"

"Well, yes, she was sad of course, and nervous about the future," said Shawna. "Why?"

"We don't want to jump to any conclusions," said Officer Dart.

"I did notice a gun near her body," offered Alex.

"Yes," said Officer Dart, "that would appear to be the case."

119

"You don't think she killed herself? Don't you think it could be connected to her father's shooting and her mother's car thing, whatever?" asked Shawna.

"It seems unlikely," said Officer Dart, "since both of those cases were accidents."

"But why would she kill herself in my house?" asked Shawna. "And she was babysitting. That doesn't seem very responsible."

"Also," said Alex. "I didn't examine her thoroughly, because I didn't want to move the body, but it looked like she was shot twice, once in the shoulder and once in the head."

"We have to wait for the ballistics report and the autopsy report to come back. But, we do have another theory."

"What's that?" asked Shawna.

"I hate to ask you this, Mrs. Bennett – but, do you have any enemies?"

Alex reached back and put his arm around Shawna. "What are you talking about?"

"Well, it hasn't escaped our notice that the victim is a tall, attractive blonde, like yourself, killed in your house."

"What does he mean, Alex? You mean, you think the murderer was after me?" Shawna began to shake and to compulsively squeeze Lex. "Oh my god, I knew it! Everything makes sense now. Yes, I do have an enemy, and she's been lurking around here, acting like she wants to help me, but I knew it! She wants me dead, she wants to steal my husband and take my baby. I'm the only thing standing in her way, she'll stop at nothing, that witch!"

120

Alex turned and frowned at Shawna. "What are you talking about?"

Officer Dart pulled out his notebook and pen. "What's the name, Miss?"

"Meredith Bennett," said Shawna.

"The Assistant D.A.?" asked Officer Dart, raising his eyebrows, but writing it down. "I've worked with her before. Seems like a pretty straight arrow."

"Don't be fooled," said Shawna. "She's a witch, she wants to steal my husband and my baby. She can't stand that I'm still young, that I had his baby, that I gave my husband a son!"

"Well, you never know," said Officer Dart. "It's always the one you least suspect. So, are you sisters?"

"She's my ex-wife," said Alex. "But this is ridiculous. She would never hurt anyone." He turned to Shawna. "How can you say this stuff? She's been trying to help you."

"Why would your ex-wife help your current wife with her new baby? Sounds a little strange," said Officer Dart.

"Exactly," said Shawna. "I didn't want her in my house, but she kept coming over. She was relentless."

Another cop came up to Officer Dart. "The scene is secure. I'm going to Office Depot to see if they have any yellow tape."

"Sounds good. Thanks for staying late, Joey."

"No problem," said Joey. "You can wait for years for a chance like this in Kenilworth. This Whitaker family is a real bonanza."

121

"Save it for the station, said Officer Dart. "I'll see you tomorrow, bright and early."

"Tomorrow's Sunday. My wife makes pancakes."

"I'll see you at 9:00 a.m.," said Officer Dart sternly. "And you two," he said, turning to Shawna and Alex, "you can't stay in the house tonight. I'll take you inside if you want to grab a few things, diapers and such. Can you stay with a neighbor?" He gestured toward the ten citizens milling around on the sidewalk.

"That's alright. We'll stay at my condo," said Alex.

"You have a condo? Where is that, sir?"

"It's in Wilmette, just a few blocks from here."

"I see," said Officer Dart. "Two time loser?"

"I suppose," said Alex weakly, as he and Shawna stepped out of the car.

"Here," said Shawna. "Take your son. I'll get some of his baby things. Then we can go home together."

"I'll need your contact information," said Officer Dart, placing his hand near Shawna's back to guide her down the walk.

"I'm sorry," she said. "I'm shaky."

"It's alright, Mrs. Bennett, perfectly normal. Take your time."

As the paramedics rumbled down the stone walk with Clara under a sheet, Shawna's eyes filled with tears. Poor Clara. She was just in the wrong place at the wrong time. Shawna had been iffy about Meredith for years, but, until recently she hadn't thought Meredith was actually unhinged. When Shawna had Lex, she must have snapped. Meredith knew that her days with Alex were finally over, that she could never compete with Shawna now unless she went full bore poisoned apple. Shawna was sorry for Clara, very sorry indeed, but there was a silver lining. Justice would be done. Meredith would finally get exactly what she deserved.

Chapter Eleven

Ah, Sunday morning, loved for sleeping in, pancakes, and a fat newspaper full of articles recycled from last year. Although she refused to read the front page story, about a child who overcame leukemia to collect old shoes for people in Haiti, Meredith was contentedly flipping through features about winterizing your garden and losing belly fat, when the doorbell rang. Setting down her coffee mug, she shot her mother a stop-sign look, stuck her feet back into their terry slippers, and scuffed to the front door.

"Detective Reed? Al?" Meredith retrieved his name as she tightened her robe to conceal her fraying nightie. Al Reed was a hair-challenged, forty-something Kenilworth detective whom Meredith had known professionally ever since he was a whippersnapper police officer testifying against speeders.

"Good morning, Meredith, um, Ms. Bennett. A situation developed last night at the home of Mrs. Shawna Bennett. I believe she is known to you, is that correct?"

"Yes, of course," said Meredith, ushering him into the living room. "Has something happened? Is she alright?"

"Yes, yes, she's fine. Sorry to frighten you."

"Would you like a cup of coffee?" Meredith summoned him into the dining room, where her mother sat toying with mushed bits of banana and soggy pancake in an effort to remain at the table. "This is my mother, Sara Greenfeld. Mom, this is Detective Reed, from the Kenilworth Police."

"Nice to meet you," said Sara. "Won't you sit down?" She picked up her tea cup and smiled encouragingly.

"No coffee, thanks. And Meredith, I need to speak with you alone. Procedure," he said to Sara, who frowned.

"Of course," said Meredith.

"I was going upstairs to get dressed anyway," said Sara. Gripping the table, she pulled herself regally to a stand and shuffled toward the staircase.

"Thank you, Mom." Meredith pushed a syrupy plate to one side and sat down. "Al?"

"A young female, Miss Clara Whitaker, died of an apparent gunshot wound last night in the home of Dr. Alexander and Mrs. Shawna Bennett."

"That's terrible," said Meredith. "Is she the one who was hit by a car last week, and whose mother was killed?"

"Yes." Al narrowed his eyes. "Did you know her?"

"No, but I met her mother briefly. I heard about the accident on the news. And her father died of a gunshot wound in that little park."

"Yes," said Al, shifting to pull a notebook from his pants pocket. "So, Meredith, Ms. Bennett – where were you last night between the hours of seven and nine p.m.?"

"Really, Al? Why? I don't get it."

"You don't have to get it. You just have to answer the question."

"Okay." Meredith tried to focus. What was he thinking? Clara was shot, and she didn't know Clara. But Clara was shot at Shawna's house. Wait a minute. "Was Shawna with Clara at the time of the shooting?"

"No. Shawna, Mrs. Bennett, was out with her husband, and Clara was babysitting. Just answer the question."

"I was here with my family. We went out for pizza, and then we dropped my daughter Maggie at a friend's house. That would be around 7:15. Then I drove the rest of us – my daughter Lucy and my mother – home for the night. It was a beautiful evening, so my mother and I took a walk around the block. After that, we came back home. I went upstairs to read, while my mother and Lucy watched TV downstairs."

"That would be where?"

"The TV is in the family room, behind the kitchen."

"So there was a time that you weren't actually with your mother and daughter?"

"We were together in the house, but not in the same room. I read for about an hour, from eight to nine."

"I see," said Detective Reed. "Tell me about your relationship with Shawna Bennett."

Meredith paused. "She is my husband's – my ex-husband's -- wife. I try to maintain a cordial relationship with her. She has helped me with my daughters, and I've been trying to help her with her new baby."

"Isn't that a little distressing, for both of you?"

"I don't know. I've been trying to do the right thing."

Al put his notebook away and stood up. "Thank you for your time."

"Al – are Shawna and the baby okay?"

"Yes, they're fine. A little shaken up, but no injuries."

"And Clara – is it a homicide?"

"We're waiting for the reports to come back. Just doing a little preliminary footwork. You understand."

Meredith walked him to the door. As soon as he left, she felt sick. She made it back to the living room couch, sat down, and stared. Sara practically slid down the banister and sat next to her.

"What was that all about?" she asked, setting her translucent hand on her daughter's thigh.

"You remember the hit-and-run in Winnetka that we saw on the news?"

"Yes, I remember. The young girl and her mother, who live next door to Alex's house."

"Exactly. Well, that girl, Clara Whitaker, was found dead last night. She was shot in Alex's house, while she was babysitting for Lex."

"Well, that's just terrible!" Sara crinkled her forehead. Then her face cleared. "Well, what was Shawna doing, gallivanting around town, just a week after having a baby? They kept me in the hospital for two weeks with you." Sara frowned again. "And why do you keep getting dragged into her messes?" She paused. "That poor girl," she said. "The police must need your help."

Even ten years ago, Meredith would have unburdened herself to her mother. She would have told her that, as unbelievable as it sounded, the police seemed to suspect her of trying to kill Shawna. And her mother would have mothered her. She would have calmed Meredith down, talked it through, and then collapsed after she hung up the phone. Having shifted the weight to her mother, Meredith could have proceeded with a stronger step. But now, Sara had her own problems. She wasn't as tough as she used to be, physically or mentally. Maybe it was better not to tell, or at least to soften the story.

"I've investigated crimes in Kenilworth before. They don't have many of them, so they like to bounce things off me sometimes, for a little direction." Meredith looked at her feet.

"So, this girl, this young woman, was murdered at Alex's house," said Sara. "That family has a definite problem. It almost seems like someone is out to get them. Three deaths are too many to be a coincidence."

"It certainly seems unusual," said Meredith. "Though there is always the possibility that they are three separate incidents. Or two."

"Yes, that's true." Sara nodded. "And the girl was killed at Shawna's house. Too bad they didn't kill Shawna!" she blurted. "Oh, I didn't mean that, not even as a joke, that's a terrible thing to say. But she has been such a problem for you, seducing your husband, ruining your marriage. And now this, with the baby – why did she have a baby, when she knew Alex wanted to come back to you? That was just evil, that's all I can say, using a child for her own ends. Well, I certainly wouldn't blame you, if you got fed up." Sara stopped, stunned. "But you didn't, of course, and you never would. You don't even have a gun, do you? And anyway," she said, shaking her head, "it was Clara that got shot. So," she said slowly, "if someone, say, went over to Shawna's house intending to shoot Shawna, but they shot Clara instead – well, they wouldn't be guilty of anything, would they? Unless it's the attempted murder of Shawna.... But Clara is dead." Sara looked confused.

"No, Mom, that's good. You've discovered a classic Criminal Law 101 hypothetical. And it happens all the time, unfortunately – some guy wants to shoot his enemy, misses, and hits a kid eating birthday cake on the front porch. Well, you can see that we want the shooter punished for killing the kid. As long as the shooter intended to murder someone, he is guilty of murdering the person he hit." While Meredith spoke, the familiar puzzle steadied her. Then her eyes drifted toward the opposite wall, but all she could see was Clara, bleeding out on one of Shawna's pastel rugs.

"Well, I'm sure no one in Kenilworth would be so foolish as to make a mistake like that," said Sara. "Except, maybe Alex – he was always a little quick on the draw, in my opinion."

"Alex was out with Shawna," said Meredith.

"What do you mean, 'out?' Like on a date?" Sara straightened up. "I knew that man was not to be trusted! Tigers never change their stripes! There they go again, running around, leaving their baby to be almost killed, and you think he's going to leave her for you.   More likely, he'll leave her for some teenager, and you'll both be in the pickle jar!"

This was more metaphors than Meredith knew how to handle.   And honestly, she didn't feel like coming to Alex's defense right now.   What was he doing out with Shawna, that was an excellent question.   But, at the moment, with Detective Reed putting two and two together and getting Meredith, she had bigger problems.

"Mom," she said.   "I need you to think for a minute.   What were you doing last night between eight and nine p.m.?"

Sara reared up in horror.   "You don't think I killed her, do you?"

"No, of course not.   You watched TV with Lucy in the family room, right?"

"Yes, I think so. Yes, for sure."

"Did you ever come upstairs during that time?"

"Well, no. I went to the powder room during the commercials, and I might have made a cup of tea – but it was 'Dr. Quinn, Medicine Woman.' We were pretty involved. You were upstairs, right?"

"Yes. I was wondering if you might have come up for a minute and noticed me, something like that. But I don't remember seeing you or Lucy, and Maggie wasn't home."

Sara looked at Meredith. Their eyes met. "That man asked you where you were last night, didn't he? He doesn't know how hard you've tried with that woman. It's beyond all common sense. And now – she's probably trying to pin this on you, you know that, don't you? She'll stop at nothing to get Alex back, lord knows why!"

130

"I don't know what she's said. She doesn't seem to be all there at the moment, I'll give you that. Post partum nuttiness, I guess."

"Well, that's just perfect. You'll end up in the slammer, and she'll have your family. Wasn't it supposed to be the other way around?"

"Not quite, Mom." When her mother put it that way, Shawna did have reason to be paranoid. If she were pointing the finger at Meredith, it could be temporary post-baby insanity, or it could be an actual scheme.

"Well, I know you didn't leave the house last night," continued Sara.

"How do you know?"

"Because you would never leave without saying goodbye, that's a given."

"Not even to go shoot my romantic rival?"

"The whole thing is ridiculous," said Sara, fluffing up like a hen. "And I don't trust that detective as far as I can throw him! Did you see how he was dressed? He wasn't wearing a uniform or a tie. In my opinion, he is very unprofessional."

Meredith sighed. "I was looking forward to a quiet afternoon at home today."

"I'm sorry, Dear, but you have to look into this. You owe it to yourself, and you owe it to that poor Clara. Someone needs to find her killer."

"You don't think it's unprofessional for me to run around trying to exonerate myself?"

"Don't be silly. It happens all the time on TV. And anyway, you didn't do it, so there's no problem. And anyone who thinks you did doesn't know you as well as I do." Sara patted Meredith's hand. "You go get dressed now, Dear. I'll hold the fort."

Meredith went upstairs. For all her bluster, she knew that her mother was worried, and frankly, so was she. She wanted to talk to someone, really talk, to a peer, a friend. Who was she kidding, the only person she really wanted to confide in and be reassured by, was Alex. And maybe he could calm Shawna down too. Asking Alex to get Shawna off her back, if Shawna were blaming Meredith, seemed unethical – like witness tampering. On the other hand, the one thing Meredith knew for sure was that she didn't do anything wrong. The more time Detective Reed spent investigating Shawna's theory of the case, the less he would spend tracking down Clara's killer – assuming she was murdered, of course. It could be an accident or a suicide. She definitely needed more information.

Meredith closed her bedroom door, picked up the phone, and dialed Alex's condo.

"Hello," said a woman's voice. "Hello? Jesus, don't bother us!"

Meredith's stomach cringed, and she threw the phone back into its cradle. Who was she kidding? The woman that answered was Shawna. Shawna was at Alex's condo. They had moved back in together.

Meredith opened her bedroom door and walked down the hall to the bathroom. She turned on the shower. The force and the heat of the water would wash all this away. She only needed herself, she could do this, she didn't need anyone's help. She would clean herself up, pull on her gray pantsuit, and go out into the world. She would figure out what the hell happened to the Whitaker family.

Jessica had so much trouble getting out of bed these days. Fatigue weighted her limbs and wrapped her brain so that, when she came home from a day of negotiating with three-year-olds and hovering under the jungle gym, all she could do was fall face-forward onto the bed and lie there inert. Last Friday, the children at Evanston Tiny Flakes Montessori had tugged self-portraits, tie-dyed tee shirts, and emergency underpants out of their cubbies and into Organic Market shopping bags to take home for the summer. With Jessica's encouragement, all of the class pets had found vacation homes, except for the Madagascar hissing cockroaches, which now rattled in a corner of Jessica and Alan's basement. Without her teaching responsibilities, she wouldn't need to get out of bed for almost three months. Maybe by then she would be feeling better, but she doubted it. It was pretty clear that she was being punished, and nothing would improve until she told the truth. But maybe that was too simple. Sometimes telling the truth only spread the misery.

"Honey, I brought you some coffee." Jessica opened her eyes to see her husband hovering in the greenery between the rubber tree and the macramé enlaced spider plants. He set the mug on her night table, on top of her bedtime book, *Harry Potter and the Chamber of Secrets.* She had hoped it might contain some wisdom to guide her through her current crisis, but she was so tired, she would read a few paragraphs, drop off, and then forget them. Anyway, it was too late -- no amount of wizardry was going to help her now.

"Thank you." Alan hadn't noticed that Jessica didn't drink coffee anymore. Just imagining the taste made her sick. She would pour it down the sink later, when she went to the bathroom -- she would have to get up eventually, she would force herself. After all, the cockroaches were depending on her. She shut her eyes again.

The phone rang. Alan picked it up, and the concerned look on his face deepened.

"My god. How did it happen?" Alan dropped onto their Amish quilt, next to Jessica's knee. "This is horrible. I'm sorry, my brain isn't working, I have to process this. Can I call you back? Yes, quite all right, you're doing your job. Thank you. Yes, have a nice day, you too."

Alan set the phone back in its cradle and turned to his wife. Pulling her pillows against the headboard, she scooted up to a sitting position and reached out to touch his hand. It was so smooth – his skin was poreless, like satin, so different from hers, dry from constant washing to protect herself from the children's germs. Of course, Alan didn't do any housework either – since Jessica's work day occurred entirely during hours that Alan was at his law firm, and he earned more money than she did, much more, he accepted her cooking and cleaning as his right. It was almost like he didn't know that she had a job. He wasn't unkind, he was just old-fashioned, like his father. Alan's hand had a muscle that curved from his thumb around to his index finger, a muscle which distinguished his heavier, male hand from a girl's. She rested her rough hand on top of his smooth one and stroked. His hands were like his father's too. As

Jessica pulled away, Alan reached out and clasped her shoulders.

"I have some shocking news," he said. "Are you ready?"

"Yes. Just tell me." Jessica frowned and crossed her arms over her chest. Things couldn't possibly get worse, she thought. This would just slide into bed with her and hide under the covers with the rest of it.

"It's about Clara," Alan said. "She was out babysitting last night, next door."

Alan was easing her into this, to help her, or maybe to help himself. "Honey, it's okay. You can tell me. Unless – did she have some injury they didn't find before, some internal bleeding, from the car accident? Is she hurt?" Jessica grabbed Alan's arms. She could feel his biceps through his taut, freckled skin, and she realized that his grip on her shoulders had tightened. What if Clara had died from the car accident – if Cece and Clara both had died? She might not be able to stand it.

"Clara was shot last night, while she was babysitting. She didn't make it. Clara is dead."

Jessica started to cry. "Oh my god, poor Clara. It's just too much, I can't take it in. What happened?"

"The police think it might be a case of mistaken identity. I didn't get the details yet."

"That's terrible, I can't believe it," said Jessica, wiping her tears. "Well, at least she won't have to live without her mother. I see it every day at school, children crying, miserable because they want their mothers. But we always tell them their mommies will be back. I can't imagine what would happen if they knew their mothers were never coming back, that they were gone forever. Maybe somehow this is all for the best." Alan looked at her. He released her shoulders. The phone rang again. "Do you want me to get it?" she asked, reaching over him. "Hello?"

"Hello, Jessica? It's Mason."

"Oh, hello, Mason." Jessica nodded at Alan significantly. "We've just heard some terrible news, about Clara. Have you heard?"

"Yes," said Mason. "The police called a few minutes ago. Awful, you're right. They say that they have a suspect, a person of interest, a lead they are pursuing. So, that's a relief, anyway. It's good to know that justice will be done. I know Clara would want that."

"Yes, you're right." Jessica sniffed. "How is Ellen doing?"

"Well, I'm glad I've got you on the line, that's what I wanted to discuss. Ellen and I were talking, and we think it makes sense for me to handle Clara's estate. I was already helping Cece before, and I have a decent idea about what's what over there."

"Yes, well, that makes sense to me – but maybe you should talk to Alan about that." Jessica paused. "What does happen to the house and everything? I can't believe Clara had a will."

"Surely not. That means that everything she inherited from both her parents now passes to her next of kin – her siblings, Ellen and Alan. Sanford's children will finally get their rightful share."

"I see. Well. I'll tell Alan, though I suppose he probably knows, being a lawyer and all. Have you thought about a funeral?"

"Yes, that's why I wanted to talk to you in particular. Normally, Ellen would arrange it all, Clara's sister and so on. But she's a bit off her game at the moment. Ellen was thinking a cremation, and then there wouldn't be any rush about the rest of it. Do you think you could handle that end of things, a funeral or memorial service, or whatever you think is appropriate?"

"Well," said Jessica. "It's a little overwhelming. I've been kind of under the weather – and this is an awful shock."

"I'm sure you'll do fine. Just talk to Reverend Whatsit over at that Kenilworth church. I'm sure he'll see you through."

"Alright," said Jessica. "I'll talk to Alan. It might be a little while, is that okay?"

"Perfectly fine," said Mason. "Ellen will be relieved to have that off her plate, that's all. Give our condolences to Alan, will you, and tell him we'll be in touch."

"I will," said Jessica. "Goodbye."

She hung up. Alan had moved to an oak Shaker rocking chair in a dim corner of the room. Behind his glasses, his eyes had flattened. "That was Mason. He wants us to handle a funeral or a memorial service, no rush. And he says he'll handle the estate. Apparently you and Ellen get everything now."

"That's true," said Alan. He stood up and sat on the edge of the bed. He had calmed somewhat, and Jessica could see that switching into lawyer mode and thinking about money helped him. She got up, stepped into her clogs, and walked around the bed to her husband.

137

"Sanford was a big deal lawyer for a long time. He must have made a fair amount."

"Yes, there should be a sizable sum, as long as Cece didn't spend it all on shoes or give it away to the opera. From what Mason said after Cece died, there should be millions."

"And you and Ellen get all of it. Just split in half?" She bit her lip.

"Yes, that's right. Unless Sanford had some other secret family – or Cece did. The children would have to come forward and claim it, of course, or the parents would, on their behalf." The color was returning to Alan's face. Jessica looked at her lap. "But I can't imagine that's going to happen, can you?"

Chapter Twelve

In keeping with Meredith's position as Public Enemy #1, the police hadn't told her much. She assumed that the crime scene at Shawna's house didn't look like a burglary gone bad, drawers tossed around and furniture upended. With the Kenilworth branch of the Whitaker family now decimated, accidentally or otherwise, Meredith decided to start her investigation with Clara's remaining relatives, if she had any. Because Clara's mother had just died, the *Tribune* might have run her obituary a few days ago. If Meredith were lucky, that issue of the newspaper would be sitting in her recycling bin.

Meredith opened the door to her basement. Bare light bulbs lit the slatted wood stairs and the cement room housing the furnace, the hot water heater, and a maze of asbestos-wrapped steam pipes that ruptured periodically and seeped most of the heat they carried into this least-used area of the house. Discreetly hidden behind the foot of the staircase, the green plastic Village of Wilmette recycling bin brimmed with newspapers and empty milk jugs and soup cans from the past week. For once, Meredith was grateful that Maggie had neglected to lug the bin to the alley for pickup.

Rifling past Friday's paper, an unrinsed peanut butter jar, and an empty orange juice can, Meredith unearthed Thursday's business section, which, for some reason, contained the obituaries. She supposed she wouldn't want to find them in the entertainment section, and "Business" sounded serious. Cece hadn't rated the featured obituary, scored by a professional wrestler named Junkyard Dog. But Meredith discovered her at the end of the hoi polloi, sandwiched between a beloved electrician and a mercifully released homemaker.

Cecelia Whitaker, 52, of Kenilworth, beloved mother of Clara, doting stepmother of Ellen (Mason Humphrey) and Alan (Jessica), preceded in death by her devoted husband Sanford. A former actress, she volunteered for many cultural organizations and reached a hand across the ocean to struggling African children with cheery letters about her own community. An inveterate collector, she was especially proud of her teapots. Services will be held on Friday at 1:00 p.m. at Kenilworth Community Church. In lieu of flowers, the family requests donations to the Lyric Opera of Chicago.

That was supposed to sum her up. But did it? Obituaries usually focused on job and family ties, and occasionally, amusing pastimes. They never revealed what Meredith most needed to know, and what might be the most important thing about them – people they had pissed off in the extreme. At any rate, she now had a list of stepchildren, which, in the absence of a recently snubbed boyfriend, could also be a list of Clara's enemies. Returning to the kitchen, Meredith yanked out the phone book for the North Shore from between a Park District brochure and a Wilmette Junior High student directory. Sure enough, Humphrey, Mason, and his wife Ellen lived on an obscure street in Winnetka only fifteen minutes away. After consulting a map and shouting last minute instructions to her mother, Meredith hurried out the kitchen door and down the path to the garage.

Meredith drove north on Green Bay Road through Kenilworth's tiny shopping strip -- a Land Rover dealership, a stockbroker, a French restaurant, and a medical spa. Turning east, she passed New Trier High School, which Maggie would attend in the fall. Heading north on Sheridan Road, she passed Winnetka's fairytale mansions, with private beaches and windows facing the lake. After a four-way stop, she coasted into the ravines, the narrow road spinning through spindly trees, the odd driveway swooping backwards up the steep forest. At last she spotted Ellen's address, her lane ascending in the same way to the cliffs of the ravines. A few lucky homeowners perched there, teetering, their side yards thickets of wild trees, their backyards dropping sharply to the lake. But, despite their enviable view, Ellen Whitaker and Mason Humphrey were not so lucky, depending how much they loved their half sister, and what they were doing last night, when she died.

Wherever Meredith parked in the driveway, she would block a black Lexus, sleek as a crouched beast. She stopped directly behind it, gathered herself, and marched down an ivy-lined groove to the double front doors. She pressed the doorbell. After a long minute, a mid-forties man answered the door. His tortoise-rimmed glasses masked his faintly pock-scarred skin, and he was dressed for a sail in a teal polo shirt, khakis, and topsiders.

"Mr. Humphrey? My name is Meredith Bennett. I'm an assistant state's attorney, and I'm investigating the death of Clara Whitaker." Both of those assertions were true, and if he tied them together to infer that she was acting in her official capacity, rather than as a loosed-cannon suspect, so be it. "I'm so sorry for your loss. May I speak with you, and your wife too, if she's here?"

"Well, I don't know. We are grieving at the moment. And we're just sitting down to brunch."

"I'm so sorry to intrude. I'm just trying to get some background information. I'm sure you both want Clara's killer brought to justice. I won't take up too much of your time."

"Alright, you can come in for a minute. But my wife isn't feeling well. I don't know if she'll want to talk today. We just found out last night, when the police called us. And Ellen hasn't slept."

Mason admitted Meredith to the foyer, a soaring space with dove-gray walls, and followed him into the living room, airy and almost empty, its lone white couch and chair facing windows fronting the lake. The view was breathtaking, ice blue water lapping against the driftwood floor, a raft on the edge of infinity. As Mason gestured for Meredith to sit, she noticed a woman sitting just outside, on a small, roofed porch projecting from the next room. The woman, petite and dark-haired, her arms wrapped

142

around herself protectively, faced away from them, toward the lake.

"Is that Ellen?" asked Meredith.

"Yes," said Mason. "She's on the belvedere. I'll get her."

"No, don't bother her yet," said Meredith quickly. "We can talk first."

Just then, Ellen turned, and Mason waved and motioned her in. Ellen's sleek, dark bob swung slightly as she slid into the room. She wore a white cashmere robe over gray lounge pants and a gray cotton tee shirt, and her perfect red-tipped toes matched her neatly manicured fingers. In her right hand, she clutched a white mug, encircled with the Winters & Early law firm logo. Despite the puffiness around her eyes, she gazed steadily at her visitor, assessing Meredith's pantsuit, her figure, and her freeform hair, and dismissing her.

"Ellen, this is Meredith – uh, Bennett, was it? She's from the state's attorney's office, here to talk about Clara – just for background." He bowed his head, like a naughty boy waiting for a slap.

"I'm so sorry for your loss, and I'm sorry to intrude," said Meredith. "Time can be important in these situations. I'm sure you understand." Meredith settled into the chair and pulled a notepad and pen out of her purse, while she waited for Ellen to join Mason on the couch. Ellen stood for a moment, evaluating her position. Finally, she tucked her left leg behind her and sat.

"What would you like to know?" she asked.

"What was your relationship with Clara?"

"She was my stepsister," said Ellen.

"Were you friendly? Did you see each other often?"

"We didn't get our ears pierced together, if that's what you're asking. She is – was – much younger than I am. And I'm a lawyer. I'm very busy."

"We did have her over for dinner with her mother, just a few days ago," offered Mason. "So much has happened, it seems like years ago." Ellen closed her eyes and then opened them again. Meredith waited. No one said anything.

"Was that the same night that they were hit by a car – were they leaving your house?"

"They were," said Ellen. "It was very sad. It's been a terrible week. We were not a close family, I wouldn't say that. But we had seen Cece and Clara more often since my father died in April. Clara was looking forward to her last year of high school. She was a typical teenager, I suppose. She could have done anything."

"Yes, with all her resources," said Mason.

Meredith looked at Mason. "Your father-in-law was a lawyer? Quite successful, I would imagine?"

"Mason is a financial planner," said Ellen. "He was handling my father's estate, at my stepmother's request."

"Those estates can be tricky, with second marriages," Meredith said. "And how long were your father and stepmother married?."

"Twenty years," said Ellen.

"Oh, so Clara was your half sister? You had the same father?"

"That's what I said." Ellen glared.

Meredith swallowed. "People want to be fair to their spouse and their children, and those things aren't always compatible. And the survivors can equate money with love, though, of course, they aren't the same thing. As a lawyer, I'm sure your father got some good advice."

"I'm sure," said Ellen. "Mason," she said, handing him her mug, "could you get me a little more coffee?"

"Certainly," he said. "Meredith?"

"Yes, I would love a cup. Just a little milk, please, if you have it, that would be wonderful." Mason hurried away. "This must be quite a shock," she said to Ellen. "I'm so sorry. I can't imagine."

"Yes, it's horrible."

"Do you have any other family?"

"My mother lives in Ohio. She used to live in Glenview."

"I see. Did you go to high school there?"

"Yes. We moved there from Kenilworth after the divorce."

"Anyone else?"

"Yes, my brother, Alan. He lives in Evanston with his wife, Jessica. I suppose you plan to talk to them too."

"I like to be thorough. I'm sure you want justice for your sister. And in that vein, strictly routine – where were you last night?"

Ellen paled slightly. "Mason and I had dinner out, just a quiet dinner at O'Neill's at around 6:30. Then we came home. I worked on a brief in the dining room, from about eight to ten. Then I joined Mason in the den, to catch the news. We were getting ready for bed when the police called."

Mason came back and doled out the coffees.

"Meredith wants to know what we did last night. I told her that I was working," Ellen said. "Here at home."

"Yes," said Mason smoothly. "We had a nice dinner out, and then we came home. We weren't really up for much, Cece's funeral was just the day before, and now Clara, my god. It's unbelievable." He sat next to Ellen on the couch and rested his fingers beside her leg. His hand looked dainty and soft, like a girl's.

"And what did you do after dinner?" asked Meredith.

"You mean at home? Oh, I don't know. I puttered around, watched TV. Ellen needed to finish up some work. The police called right around bedtime. Ellen was very upset. We both were." Meredith sipped her coffee. Ellen stood up.

"Thank you for stopping by," she said. "Do you have any idea who did this?"

"We're still investigating. If I need more information, I'll be in touch. I have your home phone, but could you give me your work phones, please, and your work addresses? Oh, and I need your brother Alan's contact information also."

Meredith jotted everything down, took a final swig of a very good cup of coffee, and stood. "You have a beautiful home," she said.

"Yes, thank you," said Mason.

"It's wonderful," said Meredith, "a house on the lake. And you're so young, too – you'll have lots of time to enjoy it."

"We do have to work hard, though," said Mason. "The property taxes will kill you."

"I don't think talking about money is really appropriate right now," said Ellen. "I'll see you out."

Meredith strolled down the hall, stepped outside and swiveled, to find the front door slammed in her face.

"You must be Meredith Bennett. I'm Alan Whitaker. Ellen told me you might be coming." Sidestepping a hand-thrown pot of pansies and a delirium of wind chimes, Meredith climbed up the porch steps and through the open front door.

"I'm sorry to disturb you. I'm sure this is a difficult time." Despite his relaxed Sunday tee shirt and jeans, Alan looked twitchy and stressed.

"That's alright. I know you want to get this investigation started as quickly as possible. I'm sure you'll understand that we're upset over here. It's been a terrible week, and Clara – it's unfathomable, that's all I can say."

Alan ushered Meredith through the living room, loaded book shelves flanking a brick fireplace, into a claustrophobic kitchen, where she tripped around a maple table and chairs. A spice rack, canisters, and small appliances cluttered the countertops, while the red patchwork wallpaper made her feel like she had been stuffed into a pioneer's aorta. Puffy from tears and under a halo of curls, Jessica Whitaker drooped over a mug of cocoa and a plate of half-eaten whole grain toast. She indicated the chair across from her and hoisted herself to a stand.

"Would you like something to drink?" she asked.

"I hate to put you to any trouble," Meredith said. "But I would love a cup of tea." Having missed lunch, she tried not to fixate on Jessica's toast. "I'm interrupting your meal," she said.

"You sit, Honey." Alan touched his wife, then filled the kettle and turned on the flame. He grabbed a loaf from the top of the refrigerator and set it near Meredith on the table. "You'll like this. It's chocolate banana. Jessica made it."

"Thank you, it looks wonderful. As Ellen probably told you, I'm trying to learn about Clara's life, and I'll also need to know what you were doing last night."

"We went to dinner, and then to the movies in Evanston," Alan said. "We left here around 5:30, we ate at the Italian Kitchen, and then we walked to the movie theater for a 7:30 show. We saw *Insomnia* – kind of a joke, since we haven't been sleeping very well. After the show, we came home to watch the news. That's when we got the call from the police about Clara."

His seamless delivery told Meredith that Ellen had prepared him. "So, you and Jessica spent the evening together."

"Yes." Alan poured water from the tea kettle into a ceramic pot and set it on the table to steep. "I work a lot during the week, so we try to have a real date on Saturday night. I'm a lawyer downtown, and Jessica is a preschool teacher at a Montessori here in Evanston."

"Winters & Early?" asked Meredith.

148

"No, that's Ellen. I'm at a small firm, Warner & Punch. Not as fancy as Winters & Early, nor as lucrative."

"But we are very happy as we are," said Jessica. She started to cry.

"I'm so sorry about Clara," said Meredith. In a snug denim skirt and a stretched-out cotton shirt, Jessica was a mess, even by farmer's market standards. Meredith poured herself a cup of tea and sliced a thick heel of banana bread onto her earth tone plate. "Were you and Clara close?"

"Not really," said Alan, seating himself between Jessica and Meredith. "But we had been seeing her more often lately."

"Because her mother died?"

"Originally, because our father died. We went to her house last week to discuss his estate, which Ellen's husband Mason is handling. He's a financial planner at Fidelity Security."

Meredith pulled her notebook and pen out of her purse. "I know that your father died just a couple of months ago, in April. An accident with a gun, the police said." She took a big bite of her bread.

"Yes," said Alan. "Of course we all went to his funeral. Then, last week, as I said -- he died without a will – kind of surprising, for a lawyer."

"I'm not surprised," murmured Jessica.

"Why is that?" asked Meredith.

"Well – I think he tried to avoid uncomfortable situations." She paused, and Alan nodded. "We had been seeing more of Sanford in the year before he died."

"It was Jessica's idea, to see him again," said Alan. "She's always trying to bring people together. She's a softie." He squeezed her shoulder.

"Sanford hadn't had much contact with Alan or Ellen, not for years. It was kind of sad," said Jessica.

"You were the only one who was sad," said Alan. "Ellen and I were disgusted. After he got involved with Cece, we hardly saw him. And then, when Clara came along, it was all Clara all the time. Ellen and I were just a bill he had to pay. Of course it wasn't Clara's fault. I'm sure that, to some extent, we blamed Cece, but honestly, his relationship with us wasn't her responsibility."

"It seems natural to resent Cece and Clara both. Sibling rivalry is real, even in a strong family." Meredith took another bite of bread. "This is delicious," she said.

"The point is," said Jessica, "that we were trying to mend all that. We invited Sanford over for dinner, and sometimes Alan would have lunch with him downtown. I thought about including Ellen, but she can be difficult, and we didn't need the drama. Anyway, Alan is his only son, and I thought they should have a relationship. Sanford had hurt Alan, but it wasn't too late. It's never too late."

"Not until someone's dead, anyway. It seems like you got in there just in time," said Meredith. "Did it occur to you that Sanford might make a will in your favor?"

"That had nothing to do with it," said Jessica. "I just wanted them to have a good relationship, for everyone's sake. It was not about money. Not everything is about money."

150

"He seemed comfortable with Jessica. Sometimes I would come home, and he would already be here, just chatting and having a drink."

"So, you got to know Sanford better, and when he died without a will, you weren't surprised."

"I think he was really mixed up," said Jessica, "and, as I said, he didn't like to deal with awkward situations. He was sick too. I don't know if Ellen told you, but he had Parkinson's Disease."

"When did that happen?" asked Meredith. "And wouldn't that make him more likely to make a will?"

"It was only about six months before he died. And nobody likes to face mortality," said Alan. "And he had a lot going on. His tremors were under control, but he was on a lot of medication. Sometimes he seemed depressed, and other times, he was flying high."

"Do you think he killed himself?" asked Meredith.

"No," said Alan. "He was crazy about Clara, she was the apple of his eye. He wanted to see her grow up, go to college, get married – all that stuff. The police said it was an accident, and I know it sounds weird, but I do think something just went wrong, and he made a mistake. He had no reason to kill himself."

"Did he get along with Cece – I mean, he'd moved on once, might he have found someone new?"

"They had been married a long time, and I suppose it's conceivable that his eye would have wandered. But, as I said, he was sick, and he doted on Clara," said Alan. "And I think he and Cece got along fine."

"What about Cece?" Meredith poured herself another cup of tea. "I understand she was hit by a car after she left Ellen's house. Were you both at Ellen's also?"

"We were," said Alan. "Mason wanted to try his new grill. It was just a family dinner."

"Oh, it was not!" said Jessica. "It was an ambush."

"What do you mean?" asked Meredith.

"Ellen and Mason were making nice, but I could see the wheels turning, they were trying to figure out a way to get Sanford's money. You see, most everything went to Cece and Clara, and Ellen felt gypped. I think she would have been happy if Cece had murdered Sanford. There's some Illinois murderers law, and if Cece killed him, she couldn't get any of his stuff. Ellen brought that up more than once."

"Do you think Cece killed Sanford?"

Alan stared at Jessica. "Honestly, I don't know," she said. "What difference does it make now anyway? Sanford's dead, Cece's dead, Clara's dead – who cares?" Jessica blew her nose.

Meredith took a gulp of tea and looked at Alan. "So, back to the dinner party. Were you there when Cece and Clara left?"

"Actually, we left first," said Alan.

"Were you parked near Cece's car?"

"Yes, she was just in front of us, on Scott Street. At least, a Mercedes with a New Trier Badminton sticker was there."

"Ellen left before we did, by a few minutes," said Jessica. "She said she had to go in to the office."

"But she was parked in the garage or the driveway, so she could just travel down the lane and turn south," said Meredith. "Unless she took a detour, ran an errand, something like that. But, presumably, when Cece and Clara were hit, you and Alan were on your way south to Evanston, and Ellen was well on her way south to downtown Chicago. And Mason was home alone." Meredith jotted in her notebook. "Cece and Clara were walking north toward their car, and you were driving south, back into the ravines. Did you pass them at any point?"

"No," said Alan.

"Not quite," said Jessica.

"I see," said Meredith. "Alan, would you mind going upstairs for a few minutes?"

Alan looked at Jessica, who was crumbling her toast into tiny bits. "Go on, Alan. I'm fine."

"I'm not leaving," said Alan, standing up. "I think this has gone on long enough. As you can see, Jessica is grief stricken. As I told the Winnetka Police, we didn't go into the ravines on the way home. We went west on Scott Street to go to Walgreens, and then we drove south on Green Bay Road. You can talk to the police if you want any more information. I wish you would check with them and let me know if they have any leads on the hit-and-run."

Meredith put her notepad and pen back in her purse, stood, and brushed bread crumbs off her lap onto the floor. "Thank you for your time, and for the snack. I appreciate it. I'll be in touch." They walked through the dining room and past the sunroom, its windows studded with spider plants. "Your plants are thriving. Someone has a green thumb."

153

"That's Jessica," said Alan. "She's good at growing things. I kill everything I touch." He flushed. "Plants, I mean."

"I'm sorry she's not feeling well."

Alan opened the front door. "Yes," he said. "It's probably nerves. Understandable, with all this. She has a very loving nature."

"I can see that," said Meredith. "She must love children too. I don't envy her, she has a tough job. I don't know how teachers do it. You don't have any children of your own – no triplets sleeping peacefully upstairs during all this?"

"No, it's just us. We would like children, but it hasn't happened yet."

"I'm sure it will," said Meredith. "Please accept my sympathies, about your sister. And thank you again."

Meredith crossed the porch and walked down the concrete steps. She would let the Whitaker family wander through her brain for a while. She was anxious to see Maggie and Lucy, and to make sure that her mom was doing okay. Her own family was complicated, but at least they hadn't killed each other yet.

Chapter Thirteen

Sara pushed the button next to the door, but she couldn't hear anything, and the knocker above the condo number was so small, banging it would be like clicking two paper clips together. Clutching a plate of cookies in her left hand, she pounded with her right fist, while simultaneously calling, "Ding dong! Yoo hoo!"

She would give them a moment. Who knew what they were up to in there. The condo was quite a come-down from Alex's house in Kenilworth, sprawled in its lot like a stretched cat. Sara didn't trust the elevator, which groaned when considering whether to ascend and lurched when it reached the third floor. The hallway felt cramped and washed-out, with a decided undertone of grilled onions. As she raised her fist to pound again, Shawna opened the door.

"Hello, Shawna," said Sara. "I thought I might find you here."

"Yes, well, what do you want? Alex is at work, and the baby is sleeping."

Shawna did not look good. She had the usual post-baby tummy, and she needed a good scrubbing. But without makeup, she looked younger and more vulnerable. Well, that was just too bad. Sara was not going to be distracted from her mission by Shawna's momentary pathos. Shawna was up to her ears in the destruction of Meredith's marriage, a lingerie-lined wolf in a dirty tee shirt. Young people underestimated older women, they thought they were cute little grandmas. Sara was going to figure out Shawna's next move. Two could play at this game.

"I heard about the tragedy, and I brought you some cookies," said Sara. "May I come in?"

"I was trying to nap – but it wasn't really happening." Shawna opened the door wider.

"Oh, my. This is lovely." After the hallway experience, like being trapped in a doggy bag, the view through the living room windows was breathtaking. The lake, endless green today and billowing, rushed toward her and then flattened into the curve of the sky.

"Sorry about the mess." Shawna indicated an explosion of diapers, blankets, and booties on the black leather couch. A pink sweatshirt hung jauntily from the corner of the giant TV.

"I didn't notice," said Sara. She wrenched herself from the tug of eternity and walked into the slot kitchen. "Why don't I make us some tea, and we can have a little visit." Fumbling in the cupboard, Sara found one mug, three cans of clam chowder, a bag of corn chips, a box of doughnuts, and what must have been the previous tenant's souvenir teaspoon rack. Sara unclasped her purse and fumbled among Kleenexes, coins, and half-used lipsticks, to unearth a baggie containing three Lipton tea bags she had swiped, for just such an emergency, from happy hour at Independence Valley. In the sink, a used mug's congealing creamer swirled in the center of the dregs of this morning's coffee. Pursing her lips, she dumped the remains, rinsed, and grabbed the clean mug from the cupboard for herself.

"I shouldn't eat those," said Shawna, as Sara took the foil off the cookies she had bought at the Jewel Bakeshop on the way over. In payment for the spritz of M&M's on his back seat when she transferred the cookies to a floral serving plate, Sara had tipped the cab driver a full 15% and asked him to return in an hour.

"Nonsense. You need sugar. You've had a shock." As Sara fussed around the kitchen filling the mugs with water and tea bags and sticking them in the microwave, then folding paper towels into triangles to use as napkins, Shawna leaned against a scrap of wall.

"It has been hard," she said. "And I'm so tired."

"You go sit, it's almost ready," said Sara, as the microwave dinged. "There, now, isn't this nice." In the absence of any sort of table, Sara set the cookies on a central sofa square and the tea on a pizza box on the floor next to it. She handed Shawna a paper towel. "So, what brings you here?" asked Sara.

Shawna stared. "What do you mean? You're visiting me."

"Well, of course. But, you don't usually live here, do you?"

"No, I don't. In fact, how did you know where I was – where I am?"

"Just call it woman's intuition," Sara said, bending to hand Shawna her mug, emblazoned with the chemical formula for an expensive new drug. "I know that someone was murdered in your house last night. Naturally, you were upset, and you turned to Alex."

"I'm Alex's wife. He's taking care of me and our baby. We're his family." The tea in her mug lurched. "How do you know about the murder?"

Sara picked up a cookie and nibbled it daintily. It was peanut butter and candy, delicious. She hoped Shawna wasn't allergic to peanuts, as so many young people were these days. The hysteria over the eruption of these supposed allergies seemed ridiculous, but apparently they were quite serious.

"Meredith told me." She let Meredith's name roll around in Shawna's ear like an oily drop of wax cleaner. Shawna flushed. "Have a cookie, Dear."

"And how does Meredith know? Tell me the truth. She shot Clara, didn't she?" It was Sara's turn to slosh her tea. "I came here for my own protection. Meredith is everywhere, at my house, in my baby's nursery. She called me today. And now a beautiful young woman who looks just like me gets killed in my family room. I told the police the truth. Your daughter has been stalking me. She's always been jealous, she has been after Alex for years. And now that I have given Alex a son, something she could never do, I think she has lost her mind." Shawna picked up a cookie, tore off a large bite, and chewed aggressively. Then her eyes widened, and she spat the mess into her paper towel. "Did she send you here? Are you trying to poison me?"

Sara placed her tea back on the pizza box. Her hands were trembling, and she felt light-headed. She had wanted to see what Shawna was up to, but this was worse than she had thought. Shawna had ruined Meredith's marriage, and now she wanted to destroy her life. "You are imagining things," Sara said firmly. "Having a newborn is traumatic. And exhausting. And then that terrible experience last night. It's not your fault, but I don't think you're in your right mind. You might have postpartum whatcha-callit." In Sara's mind, postpartum disorders were right up there with peanut allergies, but if Shawna thought Meredith killed that girl, she definitely had a problem. "You need to get professional help."

"This is not on me. I'm sorry, but your daughter is obsessed. She wants Alex, and she wants my baby. And the only way to get them is through me." Shawna flared her blue eyes and wiped her tongue with the side of her hand. Unfortunately, she might have a point about Meredith's wanting Alex, but the baby? Sara could imagine Meredith raising Lex out of the goodness of her heart if something unfortunate happened to Shawna, but that was about it. Though she did love babies.

"You know I'm right. And that's what I told the police. And now you're here." Her voice became shrill. "Are you two in some sort of coven?"

Lex started to cry. Shawna jumped up and kicked over her tea, which pooled and then rippled toward the TV. "You have your hands full," said Sara. "I'll be leaving now."

"And take your cookies with you," said Shawna. "And tell your daughter to leave me the hell alone."

"Oh, I will," said Sara. She tipped the cookies into her purse, marched around the river of tea, and walked out.

Meredith arrived home, her brain buzzing with Whitakers. Before fumbling for her key, she tried the back door handle, and the door opened. Why couldn't anyone remember to lock up? She understood that her children felt safe, that was a good thing, but, as Meredith knew from her daily grind, crimes did occur on the North Shore. At a minimum, someone might come in and steal something – the radio? Honestly, Meredith had nothing interesting to steal. Her jewelry – a few trinkets, and her medical-resident's-salary engagement ring, and her gold wedding band, thin as a coat hanger. She set her purse on the kitchen counter, locked the back door, and hurried to the bathroom to relieve herself of hours of coffee and tea, and to consider what she had learned today.

The Whitaker spouses were alibiing each other for Clara's murder -- assuming it was a murder, that family seemed uncommonly accident-prone -- but, while Alan and Jessica claimed they were together, out on the town in Evanston, Ellen and Mason were each doing their own thing in their Winnetka house. That wasn't so unusual, Meredith's family was home last night too, and she herself was alone for an hour and did not leave to kill the phantasm of Shawna. If any of the Whitakers had wanted to shoot their sister, they were a ten minute drive away, tops. They would have had to park in the neighborhood, and the police had undoubtedly talked to the neighbors to find out if they had seen anything the night of Clara's death. She would have to find out about that. A lot of folks were probably out on Saturday night, or in their family rooms in the back of the house watching their big screen TV's. One of the siblings could have slipped into the house, committed the murder, and raced back home, in half an hour, easy.

But Clara wasn't at home. She was next door at Shawna's house. It was possible that Clara had told her sibs that she would be babysitting, but they weren't exactly chummy. And if they did go to Shawna's, how did they get into the house? Clara might have let them in – Meredith would have to find out where her body was positioned, that might be a clue. Could Shawna have left the door unlocked? She was awfully nervous these days, which suggested obsessive door-locking behavior. On the other hand, she was also sleepless and befuddled, and she had left her door open just the other day. It would be completely like Shawna to leave the door unlocked and then sit cowering in a corner because someone might break in. Meredith could ask Shawna, except that she might not remember, and they were not on the best of terms at the moment. Meredith could ask Alex, but then they would have to talk about why Alex was on a date with Shawna, and Meredith didn't think she could cope with that right now.

Meredith washed her hands and headed to the kitchen. Jessica's banana bread was good, but it was hardly a square meal. She rummaged in the refrigerator for something healthy – leftover chicken, a strawberry yogurt? She had started eating strips of deli counter ham out of a zip lock bag when the doorbell rang. Wiping her mouth with a dish towel, she swallowed and fluffed her curls. After running around all day, her tinted moisturizer had worn away, and she had eaten off her lipstick back at Alan and Jessica's house. It was probably just Lucy, home from some friend's house – where was everybody, anyway, even her mother seemed to be AWOL – or maybe it was the police, here to arrest her for killing someone who was still alive. If she were ever going to shoot Shawna, which seemed increasingly possible, she wouldn't be able to hold it together to lie about it. She didn't understand how anyone did. Meredith opened the door.

It was Alex. He stood there, tall and thin and a little stooped, big brown eyes with curved, long lashes behind his doctor's specs, a goofy smile on his face. She remembered these Sunday clothes from all those years ago, six years since he told her about Shawna, five years since their marriage ended, but it could never quite end, not for her. He stood there, a weathered, graying version of the man she had eaten pancakes with on Sunday mornings for ten years, in his blue polo shirt, faded and soft from too many washings, comfortable jeans, loose in the leg but fitted round the rear, the worn loafers, a professorial cardigan carelessly slipping off his shoulders. He took both her arms in his large, comforting hands, and he pressed his smile against her resistant mouth until she gave way and kissed him back. They put their arms around each other and hugged tight. Then Alex's phone rang, and Maggie's voice called down from upstairs, "Mom, is that you? Who is it?" They broke apart, but Alex's hand lingered on her sleeve.

"It's okay, Maggie, it's just Dad."

"It's nothing," Alex said, turning off his phone.

"What are you doing here?" asked Meredith. He used to come by all the time, he would have dinner with them and do homework with the kids and kiss her goodnight, but everything felt awkward now. He

162

had moved to the condo to break away from Shawna, but he was still married, and now they had a son, and he and Shawna and Lex were a family. And Shawna had moved into his condo, which made no sense at all.

"Let's take a walk," said Alex, glancing upstairs and tugging her arm. Meredith didn't want to go with him, and she wanted to go with him so much it hurt. They walked outside together, and she shut the front door.

It was a perfect day. The sun shone, and the trees shivered with late spring blooms, small green leaves and the last traces of pink. She could smell mulch and fresh grass and the clean warmth of the air. The toe of her shoe caught on an edge of sidewalk, and when she tripped forward, Alex grabbed her. She stopped and shoved his hand away.

"Meredith, I'm so sorry. I'm so sorry for what Shawna told the police. Of course you didn't try to kill her."

"So she is blaming me. After everything I've done for her and everything she's put me through." Meredith gripped her lips together. "I can't talk to you."

"Why not?" Alex asked. He touched her arm again.

"Because I can't."

"I know," he said. "She's crazy."

"She wasn't crazy when you married her."

"No. I was crazy, and she was…."

"I don't want to talk about it," said Meredith. "Shut up." She started walking fast, but Alex kept up. "Why is she living with you?"

"She's not living with me." Meredith laughed. "I mean, it's temporary. Her house is a crime scene."

"So she's going back, like, tomorrow?"

"Yes, she's going back. She's driving me nuts, actually. They both are."

"The baby is driving you nuts. Your baby."

"Yes. He's driving me nuts too. He's a baby, he cries, what can I say? They're going back to the house tomorrow, and I will stay in the condo, like we planned. I love you, Meredith."

She stopped and looked at him. "You have to go with her."

"What?" he said.

"She can't handle this alone, the new baby, the murder, everything – she can't do it. I don't know if anyone could do it, but she certainly can't."

"I don't understand. I want to be with you. I'm trying to prove myself to you. I want our family, not – that one."

"Alex, things are different now. I didn't see it before, when Shawna was pregnant and just being – well, Shawna – but the baby changes things. He is your child. You can't just leave him to her. She isn't stable, it isn't safe."

"They'll be fine," said Alex.

"I was there a few days ago – Friday night. I found a knife in the nursery, on the dresser. A big, scary knife."

"That doesn't mean anything. She's very protective of Lex. She wouldn't hurt him. She loves him."

"Sometimes we hurt people we love."

Alex leaned over and kissed her again. Meredith's lips quivered, and she started to cry. "Don't you see, this can't be fixed? We're doomed. That baby has doomed us."

Still holding her, Alex arched back and looked at her. "We're not doomed," he said. "We'll get through this. She'll get it together."

"Really," said Meredith. "And what about you? Are you going to get it together?"

"I will if you let me." He frowned. "What do you want me to do now?"

Meredith closed her eyes and sighed. Then she opened them again. "I want you to move back into the house with Shawna and Lex. I want you to get them both through this, make them feel safe. And when everything is stable, I want you to get the hell out of there. And I want you to not touch her, and not love her, and not enjoy her company at all in any way. But I do want you to love your son. He didn't do anything. He needs you."

"Okay, I can do that. I'll do anything you want. Are you sure?" Alex peered at her.

"I'm sure," she said. "Unless she puts me in jail, in which case you're going to have to move in here with our girls, and Shawna and Lex can both go to hell."

"Okay," said Alex. "But you're not going to jail. You didn't do anything. And justice always prevails."

"That would be nice," said Meredith. "Well, I will do my damned best to make sure it does."

She walked him to the door of his Mercedes. A turquoise cab pulled up, and her mother got out. "Thanks," called Sara. "I hope your father makes it here from Pakistan." Alex handed Sara out and closed the door. The cab driver waved and drove away. "What are you doing here?" Sara asked, staring at Alex. "Your wife thinks you're at the hospital."

165

"How do you know?" asked Alex.

"Never mind," said Sara. She opened her purse. "Do you want a cookie?" she asked, tilting it toward him.

"No thanks," he said. "Goodbye, Meredith. I'll talk to you."

Sara took her daughter's arm and turned her toward the house. "Let's go in and relax," said Sara. "I'm exhausted."

"Where were you, Mom?"

"I'll tell you all about it," said Sara, "after you splash some cold water on your face and have a cup of tea. You do too much. I'd like to take care of you for a change."

Meredith nodded. Sometimes she saw glimmers of her mom, back from the past. Even though Meredith was forty-three years old and a fully-formed adult, she still needed a mom sometimes. And now, at least for this moment, she might have one. She patted her mother's hand, and they walked into the house together.

Chapter Fourteen

Meredith parked in front of the Kenilworth police station, a flat-topped rectangle with a phalanx of floor-to-ceiling windows monitoring activity across the street at the Metra tracks to and from Chicago. The officer at the front desk took Meredith back to Al Reed's office, a bland, functional room with a view of the bike path that wound through a playground before ascending to the Green Bay Trail. In a swivel chair behind an old wooden desk, Detective Reed, cradling his phone, motioned for Meredith to sit. After a few hurried thanks and jottings on his notepad, he turned to her.

"Thanks for coming. Would you like some coffee?"

"No thanks, Al. What's up?" While Meredith's knowledge of the system and of her own innocence bolstered her, she was anxious to know where she stood with the local police. In addition, she still knew very few details about Clara Whitaker's death. Although Sara had muscled her way into Alex's condo yesterday to talk to Shawna, and Meredith had talked to Alex, neither of them had possessed sufficient wit at the time to gather any information about the crime scene.

"We completed our search of the residence, and we fingerprinted a number of items that we seized from the home. Have you ever had occasion to find yourself in the nursery of the Bennett residence?"

"Yes, Al. I stopped by on Friday, after work."

"I see." Al combed a sprig of hair flat with his fingers, drummed his hand on the desk, and then looked Meredith in the eye. "And did you, on that occasion, bring a knife into said nursery? Meredith, we found your fingerprints on a big knife in the baby's room. I am going to place you under arrest for the murder of Clara Whitaker."

"What? Al, I thought she was shot."

"And why did you think that?"

"I saw it on the news. Also, you told me yourself."

"Well, we won't know that for sure until the ballistics tests come back." Meredith was about to ask about an autopsy, when he continued, "In the meantime, would you like to explain what your fingerprints were doing on a knife found in the nursery?"

"Wait, one more question. Where was Clara killed? Was it in the nursery?"

"I'll ask the questions here," said Al. "But you don't know where she died?"

"No. You didn't tell me, and the news stories just said she died in the house."

Al pursed his lips. "Well, you tell me, and then I'll tell you."

Meredith considered. She would have advised herself to get a lawyer and to say nothing. But if the police were focusing on her, they were wasting valuable time when they could be looking for the

168

actual murderer. And she might find herself in the jail cell down the hall eating a hamburger and a butterscotch sundae from Homer's across the street, instead of unraveling this Whitaker mess.

"I was trying to help Shawna. I took the baby to his room to change his diaper. While I was looking for some clean clothes for him, I found the knife on the dresser. I was surprised, and I picked it up. Shawna came in, and I put it down. I asked her why it was there, but she told me to leave, and I decided it was best to do so."

"Well, that's strange. Why would she have a knife up there? Was there any evidence of, say, a large baby gift with a lot of tape on it?"

"I didn't see anything like that, Al. She does seem kind of paranoid – honestly, who can blame her, with all this weirdness going on next door and a new baby and no sleep. Maybe she brought it up for protection?" Al nodded his head, considering. "So, was Clara shot in the nursery?"

"No." Al frowned. "She was in the family room, on the couch. The TV was on." The phone rang, and he picked it up. He grunted a few times and hung up.

"That was the crime lab. They completed a ballistics test on the bullets found in Clara's body and the gun that was found next to her. The bullets did come from that gun. And," Al paused, "it was the same gun that killed Sanford Whitaker."

"Interesting," said Meredith. "So, am I still under arrest?"

"No, sorry about that. What do you think happened?"

"I'll take that cup of coffee now, and we can talk about it. And a doughnut too – coconut, if you have one."

Al got up to fetch Meredith's snack. Although she had been trying to behave like a prosecutor, she could feel sweat drying under her blouse. She closed her eyes and took a few deep breaths. After a moment, she heard Al's footsteps heading toward her, and she straightened up.

"Here you go, Meredith. Sorry about the heat. Just doing my job."

"I understand." Eyeing her jelly doughnut – coconut had been a real flyer – she picked up her cup and took a sip. "So, do you have the autopsy report on Clara?"

"Yes. She was shot from behind, once in the shoulder and once in the head."

"So, we know it wasn't a suicide or an accident. It was a murder." Al nodded. "The killer could, in theory, have been after Shawna – he saw a tall blonde in her family room and assumed that she was Shawna. But why would someone who wanted to kill Shawna have that gun? She didn't kill Sanford Whitaker, did she?" That seemed like a crazy, but not entirely unappealing, idea.

"We checked on the gun after Mr. Whitaker's death. It was registered to Mrs. Cece Whitaker. Mrs. Whitaker kept it in a drawer in the family room, under a hand painted teapot shaped like an Egyptian pyramid, as I recall. So anyone in the Whitaker family would have had access to it."

"At the time of Sanford's death. But, what about at the time of Clara's death? What did the police do with the gun after their investigation of Sanford's death?"

Al pushed a button on his desk. "Marge, will you check and see who picked up Sanford Whitaker's personal effects, his gun, etcetera?"

Meredith took a bite of doughnut and licked the jelly off her top lip. The fried cake, mixed with stale coffee laced with nondairy creamer, should provide a nice little case of indigestion to see her through the lunch hour. Clicking heels foretold Marge's arrival. Based on her flashy red hair, her matching bright mouth, and her curvy figure, Meredith could deduce a couple of things about Marge. She enjoyed a morning doughnut herself, and she was definitely not from Kenilworth.

"I checked the files. We released all of Mr. Whitaker's effects, including the gun, to his son-in-law, Mason Whitaker."

"Thanks." Al turned to Meredith. "So. I guess I'd better talk to Mason Whitaker."

"Sounds right," said Meredith. "It's possible that he kept the gun, but more likely that he returned it to Cece. Do you mind if I talk to Mason's wife? I'm not under suspicion any more, am I?"

"No, sorry, no. Please talk to the wife. Do you happen to know where to find these folks?" Al looked at Meredith hopefully.

Meredith blushed. "Mason is at Fidelity Security, and Ellen is at Winters & Early. We can circle back later today. Just a couple more things. Why did you decide that Sanford shot himself by accident? It seems kind of funny, with him in the park and all." Meredith took another bite of doughnut and tried to look nonchalant.

"He didn't leave a suicide note, and she didn't know any reason he would kill himself. The gun was there, right next to him, it was his gun, and his prints were on it. He was shot at close range. The wife was very upset. We wanted to help her, not to cause her unnecessary grief."

"I see," said Meredith. "So it might have been a suicide, but it didn't look like a murder."

"That's what we thought," said Al.

"Another thing," said Meredith. "Have you talked to the Winnetka Police about the hit and run, when Cece was killed?"

"Of course."

"Did they talk to Alan and Jessica Whitaker, the stepson and his wife?"

"Yes. It couldn't have been them. They were at Walgreens in Glencoe. Something about a tummy upset." Al grimaced sympathetically.

"Any corroboration of their story? Any security footage from Walgreens?" Meredith figured that at least the pharmacy area must have a camera.

"Well, no. It's a good neighborhood, so Walgreens didn't waste money on a camera inside the store. They just watch the parking lot, so they can tow people who park there and then eat down the block. The Whitakers said they parked on the street. Alan Whitaker is a respected attorney. The Winnetka police think it was probably some kids from Chicago on a joy ride gone bad."

"Did anyone ever take a look at any of the family cars, to see if they had front end damage?"

"Of course not!" Al was indignant. "That is a respected North Shore family, and they have been through enough. And they knew those ravines. The daughter and her husband live there, and the son and his wife visit them, have dinner, drinks, and so on. They wouldn't have an accident like that and leave their own family members on the road to die!" Al paused. "Would they?"

"Okay," said Meredith. "Back to Clara Whitaker. Were there any signs of forced entry at Shawna's house? And, did the neighbors see anything?"

"No signs of forced entry. Dr. Bennett said that the front door was unlocked. This is a very safe community." Meredith brushed crumbs off the front of her blouse. "And we talked to the neighbors. They were eager to help, but no one had seen anything unusual that evening. The woman across the street was taking her dog for a walk when the Bennetts arrived home, and of course everyone came out when the police arrived on the scene."

"Thank you, Al." Meredith stood up. "Let's talk later."

"I'll call you," he said.

Meredith decided to hit the restroom before heading downtown to talk with Ellen Whitaker. Being momentarily arrested had been uncomfortable, but it was worth it. This was going to be interesting.

Meredith had visited Ellen's law firm before, but she was still impressed when the elevator door opened and she faced the name Winters & Early in raised marble letters projecting from the slabs that lined the elevator bank. Gripping her briefcase, she stepped through glass double doors to the receptionist's desk.

"Meredith Bennett to see Ellen Whitaker."

"Certainly." As the receptionist punched in Ellen's phone number, Meredith scooped several fun-size candy bars from the dish on the counter next to her and dropped them into her purse. The receptionist looked up. "She'll be out in a moment."

In the waiting area, Meredith sat on a leather couch and scanned a selection of business journals splayed across a glass table. After ten tense minutes, she heard a voice behind her.

"Hello, Meredith. Won't you come with me."

Sinking into the white carpet that coated the hallway like snow, Meredith followed Ellen's glossy hair, her silk blouse and slim skirt skating between a rim of closed doors and central carrels hiding support staff. Through an open door displaying Ellen's name on a removable metal plate, they entered a medium-sized office with a window facing south to Grant Park. A sliver of lake peeked out from the left. Ellen closed the door and sat behind a teak desk in an ergonomic chair with her back to the window.

"I'm busy. What do you want?" Ellen's desk was cluttered with corroborating papers. A packet of peanut butter crackers and a Diet Coke indicated an interrupted lunch.

"I wanted to tell you in person. Based on ballistics tests and her autopsy, the police have determined that Clara's death was a homicide."

Ellen flushed. "I'm sorry to hear that. After my father's death, it was hard to know what to expect. Thank you for coming by." She picked up her pen.

"Certainly. And while I'm here, I wanted to talk to you for a moment. I'm sure you want to find out who did this to your sister."

"She was my stepsister. We weren't close." Her skin was poreless, like ice. "I already told you all that I know."

"Would you please tell me again what you were doing the night Clara died?"

Ellen's gold necklace glinted in the fluorescent light. "Mason and I went out to dinner. After that we came home. I was working in the dining room, and I guess that Mason was around."

"So you two didn't interact once you got home."

"Not really. I believe he says he came in once or twice. I didn't notice, I was immersed. I had a lot of work to do."

"This is a nice office," said Meredith. "Are you a partner now?"

"A senior associate. I'm up for partner this year."

"That's a lot of pressure," said Meredith. "I don't envy you."

"I don't envy you either," said Ellen.

"Your father was a lawyer too? And quite a successful one."

"Yes," said Ellen. "What about it?"

"Your brother Alan said that he died without a will. That was surprising. I would have thought that in his situation, with children from a previous marriage and a current wife and daughter, he would have wanted to make sure that he provided for everyone fairly. Though, I suppose no one likes to face his own mortality, and the law on intestacy does a pretty good job. It's been a while since I've looked at it. I would imagine that the wife gets half, and the children split the rest equally – so Cece got half of his estate, and you and Alan and Clara each got one sixth?"

"That is the rule. In this case, most of Sanford's liquid assets, his various accounts, passed outside the estate to designated beneficiaries."

"And who were those beneficiaries?"

"Most of the money went to Cece, and some to Clara. Clara also got his life insurance proceeds. That makes sense, she was young and needed an education. Alan and I understood." Ellen tossed her head, her hair swinging in perfect alignment.

Meredith tugged her notepad and pen from her briefcase and began to write. "So, bear with me. I think I might need to diagram this. Sanford shot himself accidentally. His money went almost completely to Cece and Clara. And you all would share his personal property and the house? So Cece and Clara would have to move?"

Ellen smiled slightly. "No, not quite. Cece got the house through tenancy by the entirety. But we did get a portion of his personal property."

"But then Cece died in a car accident. I believe that happened in your neighborhood. Were you home then too?"

Ellen frowned. "No. The family had come to our house for dinner that night, and then there was a work emergency, and I had to come here. Everyone was still at our house when I left. I don't know what happened after that."

"Okay," said Meredith. She stared down at her paper. "So, with Cece dead – I don't suppose she had a will, if her husband didn't?"

"No."

"So, everything she owned, all the money she got from your father, her portion of the property and the whole house – all that went to her next of kin, which was Clara. Cece hadn't adopted you, nothing like that?"

"No," said Ellen. "We have a mother, as I told you."

"So, now, Clara has everything your father owned, except for that one sixth of the personal property and loose change that you and Alan each got in the first place. In other words, Clara has virtually all the money, the house, and two thirds of the property. Well, that certainly doesn't seem fair. You and your brother and Clara are all equally Sanford's children, but she ends up with almost everything. But now, Clara is dead. No will, I'm sure. And everything she has goes to her next of kin – her half siblings, you and Alan, fifty-fifty, share and share alike. You and Alan split everything. That seems like the fairest outcome, doesn't it? Except for all the dead people, of course."

Ellen looked at Meredith. "That's the way the law operates. What's your point?"

"One more thing," said Meredith. "Alan mentioned that you and your father weren't on the best of terms – that after the divorce, Sanford didn't pay much attention to you two."

"That was a long time ago. We're all adults now."

"So you were seeing more of your father, getting along well, family gatherings, all of that good stuff? Buried the hatchet?"

"We got along fine," said Ellen. "I had my life, and he had his." She stood up. "Do you know your way out?"

"I'll find it," said Meredith. "If I get confused, I'll call the sled dogs. Thank you for your time. And so sorry for your loss."

Poor Ellen, Meredith thought, wandering in a circle to the elevator bank. She certainly had a lot to handle right now – extraordinary family stress, and the problems that went with future partnership – all eyes on her work, the quality of it, and especially the quantity – and she was a woman, which made things even harder. And if she did succeed, it would be a hearty handshake, followed by a stick-up – she would have to contribute thousands of dollars to buy her shares of the partnership, besides currently paying for the house on the lake, that mortgage and those insane property taxes, all on an associate's salary. It was a good thing she was married to a financial planner. He must have it all figured out.

From: ewhitaker@winters.com
To: mason.Humphrey@fidelitysecurity.com
Re: Saturday night
Date: June 15, 1998

Dear Mason:

Meredith Bennet came to see me today about Clara's death. She may come to see you too. I am so glad that we were together all Saturday night. I know I was very upset yesterday. It is terrible to think about what happened to that poor girl. It must have been some kind of mistake.

I was thinking too how lucky it was that we had that cup of coffee together around 9:15 Saturday night.

Thank you for all your support. I don't know what I would do without you.

Ellen

P.S. Please delete this email.

From: mason.Humphrey@fidelitysecurity.com
To: ewhitaker@winters.com
Re: Saturday night
Date: June 15, 1998

Dear Ellen,

I just got back from lunch, and there is a police detective here to talk to me. Don't worry. See you tonight.

Love,
Mason

Chapter Fifteen

Maggie loved her grandma, but having her around all the time was getting way old. Take today, when Maggie got home totally starved, because breakfast was gross, and then when she and Ashley were shopping at Old Orchard, the jeans were, like, intravenous, so all she ate at the food court was two chicken nuggets and Ashley's fries. By the time she took the bus home because her mother refused to pick her up, even though the courthouse was practically in the mall, it was like four-thirty and she was literally dead from hunger. So, she was trying to find anything decent to eat, and all they had in the fridge was a head of lettuce and a yogurt with Lucy's germs sprayed all over it. And Grandma, who should be in Florida where she actually lives instead of in their house forever, comes sneaking in, all close the refrigerator until you know what you want, like you have x-ray vision or something. And Grandma says, it's almost dinner time, if you're hungry you can have a piece of bread, which is a test, because it's a lame snack that nobody could ever want. And even though Grandma can be really nice and was super cool about not telling Mom that she went to the sneak preview of *Bride of Chuckie* -- which is an R-rated movie even though it is not that scary and everybody there was, like, ten years old – that was on Saturday night, when a real live creep show happened at Shawna's house. Speaking of which, Maggie told Mom that she did not want to babysit for stupid Lex, and Mom made her do it anyway, and it was just plain lucky that the next-door girl was babysitting that night instead of Maggie because otherwise Maggie would be dead, and wouldn't her mother be sorry now. And then she would never be a bride, not of Chuckie, or anybody.

So, she was in her room starving, and she was just about to call Ashley to tell her about it, when Grandma screamed at her to help with dinner. And it wasn't like she was a slave or something, she was just a kid, she shouldn't have to do everything around here. She came downstairs really slowly, because she barely had enough energy left to breathe, she was totally out of fuel. But she made it into the kitchen, she was practically crawling, and there was Grandma, bossing Lucy around, and now Maggie too. Grandma was sitting on a chair lugged in from the dining room, and Lucy was stirring something on the stove, and Grandma pointed, and Maggie could practically see the magic sparkles come out of the end of her finger, "And you! Make the salad."

But the funny thing was that Lucy and Grandma both looked pretty happy about it all. And even though Grandma still looked skinny and frail, she had some spots of roses in her cheeks that might be makeup or a fever, but might also be her getting healthier and stronger. And if it was a choice between Grandma getting better here forever or Grandma buried in a bog in Florida, Maggie had to admit that she would rather have Grandma here, even telling her to peel the cucumbers, which you totally didn't have to do even though they were waxed.

So, when Mom came in the back door, which finally happened, it was so late, like maybe five-thirty, and Maggie was ready to eat even celery, Mom saw this perfect happy family of her two daughters and her old mother making a homemade dinner of chicken again and salad and macaroni thank god because she wasn't sure she wanted to eat meat ever, she would probably be a vegan next year, and then Mom smiled and looked like she was really happy to be home. And the only thing missing from the picture was the loving dad, back from a hard day earning money to buy his children shoes, when, ding dong, the doorbell rang, and the next thing you knew, Dad was in the kitchen. And now Dad had a big smile on his face, but nobody else did.

"Alex, what are you doing here?" asked Mom, when he walked into the kitchen like he lived here, which he totally does not.

"You left the front door unlocked. You should be careful about that," and he looked at Grandma. And if looks could kill, Dad would be in a body bag. "I thought maybe I could have dinner with my favorite girls tonight," he said, which is pretty ironic, considering he picks Shawna over us like all the time.

"There isn't enough," said Lucy. "We only have four pieces of chicken. So I guess you'll have to go home to your own house and have pizza with your new baby." Which was actually a pretty great zinger for Lucy, but then Dad looked sad, and Mom started talking, like, "it's nice to see you," or something, and Grandma kicked her.

Then Mom walked over to Dad, and she didn't know what to do, she just looked emotional. And Dad looked like he might take his chances, and he was bending down, so Maggie had to intervene.

"Dad, you should go home," Maggie said.

And he looked at Mom, and she nodded. "Everybody is a little upset right now," she said, which is like the understatement of the year, but she always lets him get away with murder. "And the kids are right. You need to go over there and make sure everyone is okay."

"I don't think there's anything to eat there," said Dad, and Lucy stepped up again.

"How old are you?" she said. "Pick something up at the Jewel. It's across the street from your condo, in case you haven't noticed."

And then Maggie felt sorry for him, because his condo is pathetic. And he tried to give Lucy a kiss, but she wouldn't, and he waved to Grandma, and he only winked at Maggie, even though she might have let him kiss her cheek, but he didn't even try. Then Mom walked him to the front door, and Maggie didn't know what happened there, but when Mom came back, her face was red, and she didn't have any lipstick on, but she usually doesn't, she eats it off. Then Mom went up to change her clothes, and the kids set the table and took the chicken out of the oven. And when she came down, her face was washed, and she looked clean and pretty. She rubbed Maggie's back and Lucy's, and she took Grandma's arm and strolled her to the dinner table. Everybody sat down and ate, and it was a pretty good dinner, and everyone was pretty happy. But Maggie wondered if Dad was holding Lex while he ate a piece of pizza, and she could tell that Lucy did too.

"Your girls are angry at their father. And they should be helping."

As usual, Meredith had excused Maggie and Lucy from the table to watch TV in the sunroom. Sara sat in her chair in the kitchen and sipped a cup of hot water, while Meredith rinsed the dishes and loaded them into the dishwasher. She silently scrubbed a pot, but Sara knew that stoop. Meredith could handle her prosecutorial duties and her adolescent daughters and even Shawna's nutty accusations. The weight on her shoulders was Alex.

"It's alright, Mom. I kind of like doing this, it's relaxing. I can never remember – are you supposed to rinse the dishes or scrape them?"

"Don't change the subject. You have been working all day to support this family. Are you getting any money from Alex? You were married ten years. In my day, you could have gotten alimony, not to mention child support. You're a lawyer, Meredith. Don't let him take advantage."

Meredith wiped the salad bowl. "I wasn't at work today, technically speaking. I talked to the Kenilworth police, and then I went downtown and interviewed Ellen Whitaker, Clara's half-sister. She's a lawyer too." Meredith bore down on the chicken pan with a Brillo pad.

"I'm sure the police need your help. And the case involves Alex and Shawna. You're certainly all mixed up with them." Sara stood for a moment to set her tea cup on the counter.

"I know you don't approve." The scouring got louder. "And you're right, the girls are angry at Alex. But Lucy's almost twelve, and Maggie's a teenager. They're not so crazy about me either. It's a stage, they'll outgrow it."

"I don't know, Honey." Meredith turned around to grab the macaroni pot, and Sara saw dark circles, like bruises, under the thin skin rimming her eyes. "I'm sure their age worsens things. But don't minimize their trauma. People think that, because divorce and second families happen so frequently, it's not a big deal, but this is their lives, it's a big deal to them. Their father left them, he moved out, he married someone else. They tried to adjust. After, what, four years, it looks like he might be getting sick of her, and then he moves to Florida for a year. And finally, when he comes home to try to get back to you all, bam! He has a baby. And that baby is a really big deal. He is a real human being, and he is going to be around forever. Now Maggie and Lucy aren't his only children anymore. What's going to happen to them? Will he still love them?"

Meredith turned around and wiped her hands on her jeans. "Of course he'll still love them. Nothing changes that."

"Maybe," said Sara. "But he's a busy man, and babies need attention. And Shawna needs help, and she's not too proud to ask for it."

"I'm done. Thanks for the company. Why don't you rest, watch some TV with the girls."

Meredith took Sara's arm, but she batted it away. "No, I want to talk to you."

185

Sara picked her way into the living room, with Meredith dragging behind her. When they reached the sofa, Sara dropped into it. Meredith sat next to her, meekly, like a child.

Well, she was Sara's child, and sometimes she needed direction, for her own good. And Sara held her tongue about so many things. If only Meredith would buy herself some classic pieces, good blouses and slacks, instead of, yes, she actually was wearing her maroon University of Chicago tee shirt with the Nobel Prize winners listed on her chest. And she had such a beautiful face, her hair could use a trim, it got wild – and maybe contacts. Then she would attract a new man, a better man, someone without so many problems. Sara knew she couldn't say those things, even though it killed her, because they might really help. But daughters wanted their mothers' advice about their children, didn't they?

"I just see a lot of complications here. Remember when Lucy was born, and Maggie kept smacking her in the face with her stuffed bear?"

Meredith smiled. "You don't think she was just trying to share?"

"You're a loving mother, you always think the best of your children. But no, Maggie was jealous. Sibling rivalry is natural. And it's not a stage."

"So, what's your point? Now Maggie and Lucy are jealous of Lex, and they're taking it out on Alex?"

"Something like that. They don't like Lex, and they don't trust Alex. Why should they? Why should you?" Sara tried to sit back, but if she did that, her feet would dangle. It was hard enough to be taken seriously as a senior citizen, without actually looking like a five- year-old. Meredith reached back and shoved a pillow behind her. She was always a good daughter, considerate and tactful. Either that, or she was trying to distract her.

"I don't really want to talk about Alex right now, Mom. I'm tired."

"What about that mansion in Kenilworth? Is he going to pay for that gold digger and her son to live an elegant life, while you scrape by here?"

"We're hardly suffering, Mom. I make a decent living."

"Your daughters are going to notice, they will see the difference. Sometimes money is love." Sara shook her head. Meredith was a grown woman. She must know that by now. "I mean, of course it's not really love. But people see it that way. Children are always worried about fairness, and they don't grow out of it."

"I'll talk to him," said Meredith. "Besides, he came over tonight. He wants to be with us."

"Maybe, maybe not. Tigers don't change their stripes. First he wants you, then he wants a different woman, then he flips around again. Before long, he'll notice someone new. You've worked hard to raise your daughters. I'm just worried he's going to mess everything up. I've seen it happen too often."

Sara folded her hands in her lap, a palm gripping a fist. She had seen things too. Granted, most of them were on TV or in *People* magazine, but that was just because ordinary folks kept quiet. Richard Burton married Elizabeth Taylor twice, and look how that turned out. Divorced again, and Liza Minnelli's world in shambles. Ruined lives, theirs and everyone else's.

"Do you really think I'm going to wreck Maggie and Lucy's lives?"

Oh, now she had done it. "No, no, Darling, of course not." Sara reached out and patted Meredith's thigh. "You are a wonderful mother, and they are beautiful girls. I just worry about you."

"I know, Mom. It's all a big mess now. And it is Alex's fault. But – I don't know." She looked pathetic. She didn't want truth. She wanted mercy.

"This weekend, let's go shopping, just the two of us. We'll have some fun. I think Carson's is having a Clinique bonus. We could go out to lunch. My treat."

Meredith hesitated. "If you think you're up to it."

Sara could tell that Meredith was humoring her, but that was fine. "I'm feeling very well. Being here with you and my granddaughters is the best medicine. Actually, I had forgotten how wonderful it is to be together. When you're apart, you can't let yourself remember."

"We love having you here, Mom. You're a huge help to all of us."

Sara couldn't tell if Meredith meant it. But it didn't matter. Sara knew that she was a huge help, whether Meredith had figured it out or not.

Chapter Sixteen

Tuesday morning, Detective Reed invited Meredith to accompany him for a last look at the crime scene before Shawna moved back into her house. Meredith eagerly accepted his post-arrest olive branch/cry for help, although she had of course seen Shawna's house before. The recent addition, outside the new-normal explosion of baby things, was a large blood stain smearing the peach couch and puddled on the rug below, and a red-brown dribble down the couch back and seeping into the maple floor. Clara must have been sitting on the couch when the killer sneaked up behind and shot her. There were no signs of a struggle, no overturned lamps or chairs, and no tossed drawers or missing items to indicate a robbery. The police had searched for fingerprints, bloody business cards, anything the shooter might have left behind, but they found nothing except Sanford's gun, wiped clean and dropped next to Clara's body. While Al took his final, desperate tour, Meredith walked next door to the Whitaker's house, to which the police had access with the permission of Mason Humphrey, Clara's self-appointed executor.

The first thing that struck Meredith was that everything was pink. It was like Queen Victoria's zombie's womb, dead but undead, a new house mimicking an old one. In the first parlor, rose chairs flanked a settee facing a marble fireplace, while in the second parlor a blush doily-decked sofa anchored a fainting couch and two round pale poufs. And every table and shelf displayed teapots, some classic, others almost unrecognizable – teapots high, low, everywhere.

Meredith walked back through Cece's kitchen, where windowed cabinets displayed scores of teapots of all shapes and sizes and textures, from a tiger with a tongue spout to a bone china windmill, its handle a tulip blossom. In what she supposed was the conservatory, a curved wall of windows showcased the backyard gazebo, its trellises draped with budding clematis vines. The furniture here was pink chintz and white wicker, and the glass-topped tables held, beside the teapots, a few actual signs of life – a Diet Coke can, a plate sticky with the remnants of cold lasagna, and an *Us Weekly* magazine. Through the side window, behind a table displaying a silver tea set on a silver tray, Meredith could see Shawna's house. She tried to spot Al inside, to give him a friendly wave, but she couldn't. The situation might be different at night, with the lights on next door.

Scanning the room, Meredith noticed the Egyptian teapot that Al had mentioned, on a side table with open drawers. That was where Cece had kept the gun that had killed her family. Meredith walked over and looked in the drawers. The top one contained coasters decorated with botanical flowers, and the second was empty. Al had described the teapot as a pyramid, but it was more like a sphinx, an inscrutable face with a bricked feline behind. Pyramids contained the tombs of Egyptian kings, their mummified bodies in stone sarcophagi, surrounded by jars containing their organs – their hearts, their stomachs, their brains. Meredith didn't know if a sphinx contained anything at all.

Grabbing the teapot's rump, Meredith tried to lift its lid. It didn't budge. She tried to turn it, to align an internal notch, but this also failed, as did more adamant tugging.

"Nothing knew next door," Al announced, entering the room. "Ready to go?"

"Not quite." Meredith abandoned the teapot. "When you first came here after Clara's shooting, did you notice anything unusual?"

"Only in Mr. Whitaker's office."

"Show me," said Meredith.

They passed through the dining room, a dark, ghoulish set-up -- emerald wallpaper festooned with a tangle of nightshade, a wine rug, and chairs upholstered a glossy black. A mahogany china cabinet exhibited what looked like mausoleums with spouts. Meredith hurried behind Al to an open door.

Sanford's office was the only room without a single teapot. An imposing walnut desk dominated, but its drawers were yanked open, its secrets rifled and spilling onto the floor, as if it had been raped. The built-in file cabinet in the corner had been similarly attacked, its color-coded compartments emptied, their contents splayed across the Berber rug.

"Someone was looking for something," said Al. "Hard to know if they found it."

Treading around them, Meredith scanned the papers. They appeared to be personal financial records, investment reports and tax returns, squirreled evidence of Sanford's business success.

"I can't believe this was Clara's doing. It looks like a whirlwind came through here. Someone in a rush," said Meredith.

She walked over to the fireplace mantel, showcasing what were presumably Sanford's favorite family photos. A giant bridal Cece, veiled and beaming, presided over a series of candid shots – baby Clara toddling toward her mother's outstretched arms, preschool Clara, her blonde sprout clipped with a polka dot bow, grinning first-grade Clara minus a front tooth. Interspersed were family vacation shots, older Clara and Cece in exotic locations tropical and mountainous. At the opposite end stood a newly minted New Trier senior picture, Clara a creamy-skinned echo of her mother, slim and blonde and alight with possibilities. Still upright on Sanford's desk, in pride of place, was a photo of Clara in a white satin gown – did they still have debutante balls in 1998? – with a professional updo, virginal pink lipstick, and an irrepressible glow.

That was it. In this shrine to his family, Sanford had not a single picture of Ellen or Alan. No, wait – the edge of an unframed photo peeked out from skewed papers in the desk's top left hand drawer. Pulling, Meredith was surprised to find a recent picture of Jessica, standing in her kitchen. Sanford must have taken it when he went to her house for dinner in the last few months before he died.

Meredith turned to Al. "Do you know anything about taking the lids off teapots?"

They returned to the conservatory, where she pointed to the sphinx. Al tinkered for about forty-five seconds. "There you go – it was jammed!" Several sheets of paper had been wadded to fit through the teapot's top opening. Al unfolded and lowered them, so that Meredith see. The pages were written in longhand, the letters large and shaky. "I'll be damned. I think this is Sanford Whitaker's will!"

"May I read it?" Meredith extended her hand.

"Sure," Al said. "You're the lawyer. Just tell me what it says." Meredith lowered herself onto the wicker couch.

This is the Last Will and Testament of Sanford Whitaker, Esq. Etc., etc. I am of sound mind and body. Etc., etc.

Sanford was clearly not a trusts and estates lawyer. She assumed that this was a draft, and the etceteras referred to the usual legalese boiler plate.

To my beloved wife Cece, I leave our house, which she receives via tenancy by the entirety, and the accounts for which she is the beneficiary, as I have previously established with the respective financial institutions. I also leave her all of our personal property, with the exception noted in Clara's bequest below, especially the contents of our Kenilworth home. Etc., etc. I want her to know that I love her very much.

To my beloved daughter Clara, I leave all of the accounts for which she is the beneficiary, as I have previously established with the respective financial institutions. I also leave her my life insurance proceeds. I hope she will use the money wisely to pursue appropriate educational opportunities, preferably at an Ivy League school.

Finally, I leave her all of my personal mementos, including my watch and all of my mother's jewelry. I love her very much, and I want her to know that she is the light of my life and my proudest accomplishment.

I also leave Clara my last bit of fatherly advice, which I hope she will take to heart. Avoid your sister Ellen, to whom I leave nothing. She is a dark and angry force who can only do you harm.

Finally, to my son Alan, I leave the remainder of my estate. This includes all of my capital in the law firm, which is a sizable sum, all of my private equity holdings, and any other accounts of mine for which I have not designated beneficiaries. It is my wish that Alan and Jessica will use this money for the benefit of her firstborn child. Etc., etc.

The last page was signed Sanford Whitaker, Esq., and dated April 1, 1998. It was not witnessed. "He made this will just before he shot himself," said Meredith. "It leaves Cece a little better off, in that she gets all of his personal property. I'm sure that would have been a relief to her. The biggest change is that he leaves a chunk of money to his son Alan. And nothing to Ellen. But it wasn't witnessed. Legally, it doesn't change anything. If the family knew about it, they could choose to comply, but they wouldn't have to. Interpersonally, though, it might mean a lot, especially to Alan and Ellen."

"So, who stuffed it in the teapot?"

"I don't know. If Sanford shot himself by accident, he would have left it in his drawer. If he had lived, he would have brought it to work to have it done up properly, but he never had the chance. If he

194

were murdered, it would also still be in the drawer – unless he were murdered over the will, in which case, why save it at all?"

"He wasn't murdered," Al said.

"Right," said Meredith. "And if he killed himself on purpose, he would probably have left it on top of his desk for Cece to find. But if she knew about it, she probably would have told Mason. Of course, Mason might not have wanted Ellen to know about it, because it would upset her. Maybe Mason told Cece that he would throw it away, since it wasn't legal, but she decided to save it, just in case it came in handy – say, if Ellen and Alan were giving her a hard time about dividing the personal property. And it was her husband's wish – it would have been hard to toss it."

"Kind of dramatic, to hide it in a Sphinx."

"Her obituary said she was an actress back in an earlier life. Maybe she kept her theatrical flair."

"I'll take it in and check it for prints," said Al. He took the papers from Meredith and put them in his jacket pocket. "Are we done here?"

"Yup," said Meredith. "I guess Shawna Bennett can move back into her house. And the Whitakers can divide the teapots."

"I'm sorry I'm late. What a beautiful table!"

"No, it's fine." Jessica blinked a few angry tears from her eyes. "I was worried you weren't coming. I tried to make it nice."

She had been cooking for hours, well, three hours, and after a trip to the Jewel for asparagus and tiny potatoes and fresh flowers. She had tucked snips of fresh rosemary and lemon slices under the skin of a small chicken, roasted the potatoes, and composed a green salad. Dessert had taken the most time, apple pie with a homemade crust, and Homer's ice cream, butter pecan.

They fought last night because Alan wanted to talk to a criminal defense lawyer, and Jessica wanted to leave it alone, and when he was late tonight, she thought he might have left her. Husbands dumped women with a lot fewer problems than Jessica had, women whose only mistake was to grow older and too familiar. Since last March, Jessica had lived aslant, the earth's table tilting beneath her like a three-wheeled skateboard. All she knew how to do was to bake a pie, grab Alan's shoulders, and cling.

Alan set down his briefcase. "I'm sorry. I got caught up in some work, and you know, the el. I should have called. You look pretty." He gave her a peck on the cheek. "We can eat right now. He pulled out his chair."

"No, you change, it's alright." The chicken sat on the counter, golden and cooling, but the potatoes were black, the asparagus limp and stringy. But the apple pie sat under a checked dish cloth, like a picture. She pulled a bottle of Chardonnay from the refrigerator and opened it with their old corkscrew, a wedding gift from a college friend. She was twenty-four when they married, and Alan was twenty-seven. They had felt so hopeful then, two sparkling new adults. Now, five years later, she felt ancient, smashed by the weight of her secrets.

Alan stepped back into the kitchen and spun her around. He kissed her on the lips, lightly, too lightly, like her mouth was a habit in his path. But he did crouch down and smile into her face. "This really looks nice. Thank you."

He sat at the table where they had eaten a thousand meals, and she made two plates, first one for him with white meat, and then one for herself with drumsticks and wings. She loved the crunchy skin and stripping the meat from the bones with her teeth, but now she wondered if that carnality disgusted him, as he calmly carved a hint of fat from the breast and set it to one side.

"I'm sorry about last night," Jessica said. "You're the lawyer, you know best. I'm just frightened."

"I know you are, but I told you, I will take care of it." Alan sliced a potato and chewed a neat bite.

"I can't let you do that. What's the point? We're still lying." Jessica picked up her wine glass and gulped. They would discuss this calmly, not like last night. He had taken her by surprise, wanting to go to a lawyer, and then, possibly, to the police.

"They'll check with Walgreens, and then they'll know we weren't there. They could still find out we had the car repaired. I can't believe they haven't already."

"We took it to Rogers Park."

"Honey, that's not the ends of the earth. I can't live like this, always worrying that the truth will come out. We weren't thinking, we were upset, we didn't do anything wrong, not really. It was an accident, that's all. We'll just talk to a lawyer, that's

197

the first step. Maybe he can investigate a little, find out what the police know."

"But, Alan, it's me, I was driving." She tried to cut the asparagus, but the stem squashed under the pressure of the knife. Everything was ruined. She put down her fork and folded her hands in her lap.

"We won't turn ourselves in unless the police are almost there. And it wasn't your fault. I shouldn't have let you drive. I think talking to someone will help us."

"How can it help? I killed Cece. It was an accident, and I should have faced it. I wasn't thinking straight. I just wanted to get out of there."

"I know," said Alan. "Of course I know, I agreed with you. But now I see that we need to talk to a lawyer. You're my wife, I love you, I'm going to take care of you. What does it matter whether I was driving or you were?"

"I don't like it, Alan. But we can talk to a lawyer, if you insist." Jessica wiped her nose and reached for her wine glass. "Is your dinner okay?"

"The dinner is great. You should eat yours."

"I will." She picked up a drumstick and set it down again. "Alan, I feel terrible, frumpy and half crazy, and you seem so together, even with all of this. All those women at work, they're smart and put together, and making you feel important, not fighting with you." Jessica wiped her fingers with a napkin and tugged at her jumper.

"None of that matters. I love you." He spoke firmly but automatically, his practiced response to a standard tale of woe. "I'm the one who should be worried. I hope you don't have a guy on the side." Alan chuckled.

Jessica flinched. The idea of female subordinates flopping all over Alan was par for the course, but that a man might be attracted to her – well, he knew that was ridiculous. He looked so comfortable, chewing his homemade meal after a stimulating day in the big, important city. He said he loved her, that he would protect her, but he knew she couldn't let him take the fall for her mistake. Maybe going to a lawyer was the first step in his plot to get rid of her, to free himself to live in a bachelor pad with a girlfriend in a Velcro dress he could whip off in one clean motion, like a child opening a present. How could he look so smug, when she was churning inside? It was all a joke to him, she was a joke. Well, she knew how to turn his grin upside down.

"I've been so anxious." Jessica stood to clear their plates, hers untouched, his licked clean. She set the pie on the table, apple, his favorite. She turned her back to reach for two earthenware dessert plates and rummaged in a drawer for a pie server. "I know you've been trying to protect me. Well, I guess we're a perfect pair. Because I've been trying to protect you too." She concentrated on cutting the pie into two neat wedges. Serving the first slice was always difficult. The bottom crust stuck to the pan, and the filling wanted to slide onto the table. After that first step, the rest of the pieces would come out neatly. She kept the broken mess for herself and gave Alan a perfect triangle.

"Protect me?"

Jessica swiveled to grab the pint of ice cream from the freezer and went back to the drawer for a scooper. "Why did you have to start up with your father again? And why did he have to come here, to our home? You could have had lunch downtown, at your club – don't you have clubs for things like that?" She dug the scooper into the hard ice cream and twisted her wrist.

Alan frowned. "I thought you wanted us to reconcile, and that you wanted to be a part of it. You were so nice to him, so kind and hospitable, and he was really warming up. And now, I'm so glad we did that – who knew he was going to die so soon? It was a stroke of luck, really, the timing, it was like a miracle."

Jessica plopped a sphere of butter pecan next to Alan's pie. The dessert was perfect, it could have been in *Bon Appetit* with the addition of a sprig of mint that no one would actually eat. She pushed it toward Alan like a Roman empress serving her husband tiramisu laced with arsenic.

Turning her back, she reached up to a high shelf for a teapot. Why did people make teapots anymore? No one used them, they just zapped a mug in the microwave and dipped in a tea bag. Cece had loved teapots. Maybe they represented a civilized ritual, from a time of courtly manners that she wanted to revive. Or maybe she was just bored and needed a hobby, and the world was awash in teapots that no one else wanted. At any rate, Cece was dead, Jessica had killed her. And that wasn't the only death Jessica had caused. Stupid, dumpy little Jessica had become a tornado of doom in the Whitaker family, a spinning force of nature that nobody could stop.

She set the teapot on the table. It didn't go with anything in the house. They were Evanston people – they liked clay and earth tones and futons and fireplaces with actual wooden logs in them. The teapot was white porcelain encrusted with pink rosettes that swirled around its body, and with a knob on top shaped like an exotic green fruit. She removed the lid. "I haven't seen that for a while," said Alan. "Was it a wedding present?"

"Yes," said Jessica. "It was from Sanford. Cece must have picked it out. It's awful."

Poor Alan. He was trying. Should she put the lid back on and leave him in peace, or should she tell him the truth? Well, Alan insisted that this was a time for half truths. Half the truth would be something, and maybe it should be everything. Jessica reached into the teapot and pulled out an envelope, slit open at the top. She handed it to Alan.

He looked at it. "It's addressed to you. What is it?"

"Just read it," she said.

Alan pulled a piece of paper out of the envelope and opened it. The handwriting was shaky, but legible.

April 1, 1998

Dearest Jessica,

Spending time with you and Alan has been such a gift these last months. I was so depressed after my Parkinson's diagnosis, and the drugs I've been taking make me feel a little crazy sometimes. I love Cece, and I love Clara, but I also love Alan, and I love you.

On their death beds, old men tend to express regret that they did not spend more time with their families, and I am no exception. I should have taken better care to include Ellen and Alan in my life after my divorce – and especially Alan, as my son. I see that now. If I had done that, if I had lived my life differently – but I accomplished some good things too, and I hope that people remember those and don't dwell on the rest.

Alan is my son, I know that now, I should have treated him better, and I am starting today. I left a draft Will on my desk, and it leaves some money to Alan, and, by implication, also to you. Although I am too distraught to complete all the legal technicalities,

It is my last wish that you and it is my hope that knowing my intentions will help those I love, at least in some intangible way. Alan enjoy your first child. I know that Alan will be a wonderful father, and of course you will be a beautiful, loving mother. I just can't deal with my mistakes.

Darling Jessica, I thank you. Please forgive me.

Love,
Sanford

"What is this?" asked Alan. His ice cream was an oozy beige puddle next to his pie. "I don't understand."

"I got it the day after he died. He must have mailed it and then shot himself."

"Why did he send it to you? Why didn't you tell me?"

"I don't know, I was upset. I was horrified that he died, and sad. I don't know why he sent it to me, but he did, it was my letter, and I took it that way. He wanted me to see it, only me, and then he died."

"But still, this is big – first of all, it's a suicide note. That has implications, legal implications."

"Like what?"

"I don't know – the police would have wanted to see it, to close the case."

"But they did close it, Alan. They probably knew it was a suicide anyway -- who accidentally kills himself in a park? But they were trying to spare the family, and so was I."

"Okay," said Alan slowly. "But what about this will he's talking about? Nobody found one. He wanted us to have some money."

"Well, I thought about that. He probably did leave it. Or maybe he didn't really do it, maybe he forgot. I don't know. He obviously wasn't thinking clearly, he said so himself. And this paper isn't a will, it has no legal effect, right?"

"That's right," said Alan. "And it probably isn't worth dredging up now, with Cece and Clara both dead and everything going to Ellen and me anyway. It wouldn't be worth it to upset Ellen for a little extra money. Do you think Cece found the will and got rid of it?"

"I don't know, she might have. But, as you said, it doesn't matter. She's gone."

"Because you killed her," said Alan.

Jessica stepped back. "That was an accident, and you know it. I had no reason to want her dead, and I am not a killer. You know that, right? I am not a killer."

Alan stood up and walked around the table to her. "I'm sorry, I know that. Of course I know that.

You're the most loving person in the world. Of course my father turned to you in his hour of need. I'm just surprised, that's all. And probably a little jealous."

Alan reached out and hugged Jessica. She rested her head on his chest. "I'm sorry I kept that from you – and I'm sorry I showed you. I was torn."

"It's alright. I'm surprised you were able to keep quiet about it. You have a lot of inner strength."

"I read in a magazine that it's good for married people to have their own lives, their own secrets. You have that whole life at work, an important life that I'm not a part of, that I'll never share, even though I'm your wife."

"Well, so do you – your little tikes."

Jessica shifted uncomfortably. It sounded so uneven. But she did have a secret, one that she would always keep.

"There is one more thing. Something important. I hope it makes you happy." She arched back from him, but stayed in his arms. "I'm pregnant -- three months." She would fudge it a little, just by a couple of weeks.

"Wow! That's wonderful!" He sounded stunned, but he gave her a firm kiss, like he meant it. She could feel the tingling in his arms and the beating of his heart. It was wonderful. He was thrilled. Or he would be. "Why didn't you tell me sooner?"

"I don't know, I had a lot on my mind. It's been a terrible time. And I didn't know how you'd react."

"I'm very happy, Darling – shocked, but happy. And, not that it's a big thing, but it's nice to know that Dad would have been pleased too. Maybe we could name the baby after him – Sandy or something. After all, we live near the beach."

"We'll see," said Jessica. She leaned over and picked up Sanford's letter and stuck it back in the envelope. "Should I just put this back in the teapot?" she asked.

"Sure," said Alan. "It's as good a place as any. I'll put it back on that high shelf, and we can forget about it."

"Do you still think we should talk to a lawyer? I mean, what if one of us has to go to jail? And with the baby and everything."

Alan considered. "Well, maybe not, after all. You're right, it was an accident. They can't prove drunk driving. All we did was leave the scene, and it wouldn't have made any difference if we'd stayed. I probably worry too much, it's a professional hazard. Now we should move on with our lives, look forward, think about the baby, the future of our family."

"That sounds perfect," said Jessica. "I'll get us some fresh ice cream. I might have a little appetite now."

Chapter Seventeen

After a bolted burger at Homer's, where she resisted the sundae she would have requested had Detective Reed imprisoned her, Meredith and Al drove across the border to Winnetka. According to her secretary, Ellen Whitaker had stayed home from the office today to recover from the emotional trauma of her tragic family situation. While Meredith couldn't feature Ellen's confiding her feelings to her underage secretary, she was astonished that Ellen had for any reason decided to skip work on a Tuesday. Maybe the steady drip of disaster was finally drowning her -- whether in guilt, grief, or panic, remained to be seen.

At Meredith's request, Al drove his unmarked SUV north on Green Bay Road to the Walgreens in Glencoe, then east on Scott Street, where the Whitaker tribe had parked their cars on the night that Cece died. Turning south on Sheridan Road, he headed into the ravines from the northern end. Meredith scanned the west side of the snaking lane where Cece and Clara had hustled to their car that night.

"Not much room to walk, no real sidewalk, and no streetlights, either. And the road is so curvy. It would be easy to hit someone walking in the street, which Cece might have done to protect her shoes," said Meredith.

"Clara said they were on the path, but it is narrow. If some intoxicated Chicago teens were exceeding the posted speed limit, they could have veered off the pavement into the victims," said Al.

"Or if anyone were drunk or speeding. Did Clara remember anything about the car that hit them?"

"No," said Al. "But the case will remain open while we pursue all possible leads."

"That's a comfort," said Meredith. "I hope it was an accident. If it weren't, then somebody wanted Clara and Cece both dead. Which, although it took two tries, is exactly what eventually happened. Which suggests a family member, as does the use of Sanford's gun to kill Clara – oh, here's the place." Al pulled into Ellen and Mason's driveway and parked in front of the garage.

They had discussed their strategy over lunch. Yesterday, while Meredith talked to Ellen, Al questioned Mason in his office at Fidelity Security. Mason confirmed that he had picked up Sanford's personal effects, including his gun, from the Kenilworth Police after his death, and that he had returned everything to Cece. He reiterated that he had been out to dinner, and then in the house with Ellen on Saturday night when Clara was killed. He said that he remembered poking his head in to check on Ellen a couple of times while she was working, and that they had even had a cup of coffee together in the kitchen at one point. Ellen hadn't mentioned this coffee klatch to Meredith.

"The obvious motive for killing Clara is money. And the people who benefit from her death

207

are her half siblings and their spouses. The motive had to be money," said Al. "Why else would someone kill an innocent girl? Mason Humphrey is all caught up in the financial angle. And look at his job – it's money, pure and simple. And what if he was lying, and he never returned the gun? What if he was lying about the cup of coffee? His wife was working, absorbed, keeping her head down, she wouldn't know if he left and came back. That gives him motive, opportunity, the weapon. So, why are we here, talking to the wife?"

"Well, it's easier – she's on the North Shore today. And I just don't like her," Meredith admitted. "If we need to, we can talk to Mason afterwards."

They tromped down the ivy-lined walk to the double front doors and rang the bell. After a moment, Mason answered. "Good afternoon, Mr. Whitaker," said Al, neatly recovering from his surprise. "Nice to see you again. I believe you have met Ms. Bennett?"

Mason nodded. He was dressed casually, in a navy polo shirt, khakis and penny loafers. Crocodiles frolicked around his fabric belt. He brushed a wisp of hair from his face and frowned. "Hello. Were we expecting you?"

"We're sorry to interrupt at this difficult time. May we come in? We just have a few questions, to help us get justice for Clara." Meredith felt a wave of genuine sadness for Clara Whitaker. She was so young, just a few years older than Maggie. She hadn't done anything yet, except play badminton and learn algebra and shop. And someone shot her in the head. And the provocation had nothing to do with Clara's behavior, nothing at all.

"Well, alright, just for a moment." Mason shepherded them down the soaring hall to a slant-ceilinged room with dove gray walls and a conference room table. At its head sat Ellen, surrounded by papers and holding a tiny cup of espresso.

"I'm eating my lunch," she said. "What do you want?"

Meredith searched for signs of food, then noticed a sliver of lemon peel on the miniature saucer. "So sorry," she said. "Have you met Detective Reed? He would like to talk to you, just for a moment, we know you're busy. Mason, might we go into the other room and leave these two to chat?"

Ellen widened her eyes at her husband, but he ducked his head and led Meredith down another long hallway, through the slate kitchen and into the family room. Through its windows, the waves of the lake sparkled and flashed. A tuna sandwich bordered with green grapes, a folded napkin, and a glass of iced tea sat on the glass table in front of a sway-backed leather couch. Meredith perched on one side, facing the large TV nestled in a sleek armoire. Swiveling to face Mason next to her, she wedged her right knee under the table to keep her body from sliding sideways into the gully.

"Sorry to interrupt your lunch," said Meredith. "Please eat."

"May I offer you some refreshment?"

"No thank you. What are you doing home today?"

"I'm trying to support Ellen," said Mason. "Of course, this is all quite difficult. We would like to plan Clara's funeral, get on with our lives, but...." He shrugged. "Maybe the detective can tell us when the body will be released."

"Yes," said Meredith. "I don't know about – that -- but I believe that you will be able to get into the house shortly. I'm sure you'll want to go through all Sanford's papers, though Cece probably showed you most of them after he died. Are you handling all the financial arrangements for the family?"

"That has been the plan thus far. Of course, I have the expertise."

"Makes sense," said Meredith. "And you have a little more distance, not being a Whitaker yourself. Is Ellen quite upset?"

"Yes, of course. It's all very sad. Clara was so young." He picked up half a sandwich.

"You know, I was in the house this morning. It's in very good condition – lucky she was killed next door. No blood in your house, saves a lot of bother and distress. It is your house now, isn't it?"

"Yes," said Mason. He put his sandwich back on the plate. "Well, it's Ellen and Alan's. I hope you don't think anyone's happy about this."

"Of course not. Though it is quite a bit of money."

"I suppose. I hadn't really thought about it."

"I find that a little surprising, considering your business and the extent of your expenses. It's only natural. But, about the house. As I was saying, it was quite neat, except for the normal teenage detritus, a few dirty dishes, that kind of thing. Oh, and Sanford's study."

"What about his study?"

"You must have been in there before, helping Cece after Sanford's death. How did they keep it? Decent filing system, that sort of thing?"

"Yes, it was neat enough. Cece liked the house to be presentable. Did Clara make a mess in there? I hope she didn't spill anything – soda, awfully sticky."

"No, no wet spots. Did Ellen help you gather up Sanford's papers? Had she ever been in his study before?"

"No, not to my knowledge. Ellen was quite busy with her own work. And we weren't particularly friendly with that part of the family during Sanford's life. He didn't make an effort." Mason pursed his lips.

"I see," said Meredith. "No, it wasn't sticky. But there were papers everywhere, drawers emptied onto the floor. It looked like someone was searching for something. I wonder what that could be."

"I don't know," said Mason. "I had full access to those papers. I never found anything peculiar."

"Maybe they were looking for what you didn't find. Wasn't it strange that Sanford didn't have a will? He was a lawyer, he was sick, he had dependents."

Mason turned pale. "People don't like to face facts."

"So, you would be surprised to learn that Sanford made a draft of a will, in which he left the remainder of his estate to his son Alan? You never saw that document?"

"That draft had no legal effect," said Mason. "For all practical purposes, it didn't exist. I advised Cece to put it in the desk drawer and forget about it. And as far as I know, that's what she did."

211

"Did you tell Ellen about it?"

Mason flushed. "Of course not. It could only hurt her feelings."

"So, she was left to imagine that her father, a lawyer who should have made a will, might in fact have made one, and that it might have been overlooked or hidden somewhere in his office. And if there were a will, her father might have left her something – a bequest, however small, to show that he loved her. And maybe some money, which is always helpful."

"Maybe. She was quite upset when he died. And then Cece – well, widows can be self-absorbed. But she acted like Ellen wasn't even family. It was hurtful." Mason picked up a grape and popped it into his mouth.

"Would you say that Ellen was angry at Cece and jealous of Clara?"

"I don't know about jealous. You've met Ellen. Mainly angry." He ate another grape. "All entirely understandable, of course."

"What about you – were you angry on her behalf?"

"Not really," said Mason. "I have tried to help Ellen, of course, but I'm just an in-law. My relationship with Cece was cordial and professional."

"You were good to the family – holding that barbecue, including Cece and Clara – that was unusual. Really above and beyond."

"I thought a casual dinner might help everyone. We were going to invade Cece's house and split up Sanford's personal property. That could create some hard feelings. I was trying to ease the situation. Of course, it took an unfortunate turn." Mason took a sip of tea.

"Yes," said Meredith. "So, Ellen left the dinner, and then Alan and Jessica, and then Cece and Clara – all in quick succession?"

"Fairly quick, I suppose. The party broke up."

"And it was a party – some drinking and so on."

"A bit," said Mason. "Ellen didn't drink much of anything, she likes to keep her wits about her, and I had to cook. Alan and Jessica were helping themselves, I really didn't keep track."

"And Alan and Jessica – what were their feelings about Cece and Clara?"

"I really don't know," said Mason, setting down his glass. "I do know that they are good, straight-forward people, rice cakes, farmer's markets, that sort of thing."

"Any money problems?"

"Not to my knowledge," said Mason. "You would have to ask them. Is that all?"

"Almost," said Meredith. The coffee table was digging into her leg, so she decided to face forward on the couch and let gravity pull her back. She found herself staring at the opaque face of the television set.

"So, the night that Clara was killed, you were here, in this room, watching TV. And Ellen was working in the front of the house, where she is now, but you ran into each other, even had a cup of coffee together that evening."

"That's right," said Mason.

"Okay, that's all. Thank you for your time."

Meredith stood, and she and Mason walked into the dining room, where they found Detective Reed sitting at the table in front of his notebook and Ellen pacing around. "Everything okay in here?" asked Meredith.

"Everything's fine," said Al. "I was just asking a few questions, and Mrs. Humphrey here was insulting the Kenilworth Police Department."

"You barge into our home and ask the same questions over and over. We are grieving, and you don't know what you're doing. Just leave us alone!" Ellen was almost shouting.

"We're so sorry to bother you," said Meredith. "But this was very helpful. Your husband told us a lot about your activities on Saturday night, things I hadn't heard before. The picture is starting to become clear. When I ask myself who had a motive to kill Clara, well, there are a few of you, but then who had the opportunity – that lets us zero in."

"What are you talking about? What did you tell them, Mason?"

Mason backed up. "I didn't tell them anything."

"Because if you want to know who had opportunity – as I told Detective Reed for the umpteenth time, I was working here all evening. Mason checked on me a few times, or so he says, but I never saw him. I never saw him, not once."

"That's strange," said Meredith. "Because Mason said that you two had coffee together."

"Well, we didn't. I don't know why he would lie about that. There was a two hour period when I never saw him."

"Is that true, Mason?" asked Meredith.

214

Mason was bright red. "She told me to say we had coffee, so I said it. The truth is, I did peek at her, just before eight, but I never saw her from eight to nine. I was watching TV, I was absorbed. I always watch TV at eight on Saturday night. It was *Dr. Quinn, Medicine Woman.* I can tell you the plot, if you want."

A cell phone rang, and Al reached into his pocket. "Excuse me a minute," he said.

"Would you have heard Ellen, if she drove away and came back?" Meredith asked Mason.

"No," he said. "The family room is far away, in the back. And I was very involved."

"You are a wimp," Ellen said to Mason. "You've always been a wimp." She turned to Meredith. "I'm telling the truth."

"And when I saw her at nine o'clock, she was frazzled," said Mason. "She said that her father never loved her, he only loved Clara." He turned to Ellen. "I didn't know what had prompted this outpouring, it was childish, but it was sad and sweet. I thought it was good, that her feelings were finally coming out. You can't keep things bottled up forever."

"Apparently not," said Meredith.

Al came back in. "We found the will, by the way," he said to Ellen. "In the teapot. Your fingerprints were on it."

Ellen turned white. "That doesn't prove anything," she said.

Meredith turned to Ellen. "So, you went to Clara's house on Saturday night. Maybe your reasons were legitimate, maybe not. But when she wasn't home, you decided to look for Sanford's will.

Because you didn't trust Cece to be honest, and you didn't trust Mason to be competent."

Mason sniffed.

"And low and behold, you found it in the desk drawer, where Cece left it. And if you didn't know before that Clara was Sanford's favorite daughter, you certainly knew by the time you left his study." Meredith paused. Ellen's face was white and bloodless, her right hand clenched. "So, the will in your hand, you went into the family room for the gun. You weren't sure what you were going to do with it – maybe wait for Clara, maybe even go after Alan, who knows what -- and then you had a surprise. Through the window, you spotted Clara next door. So, in a jealous rage, you jammed the will into the teapot, ran over to Shawna's house, and shot Clara."

Ellen stared at Meredith. "Go after Alan?"

"You didn't read it through?" asked Meredith. "After all of that, you stopped after the bequest to Clara?"

"What did it say?" asked Ellen.

"It wasn't legal," said Meredith. "It wasn't witnessed."

"But what did it say?" shouted Ellen.

"Your father left everything else to your brother Alan. For the benefit of her firstborn child. Jessica's," said Meredith.

"Those were the words, 'her firstborn child?'"

Meredith nodded.

"Why would he say that? Why the hell would my father care about Jessica's first child?"

"Apparently Alan and Jessica had been spending quality time with Sanford during the past year. They'd been inviting him for dinner. Sometimes he had lunch downtown with Alan. And sometimes he would come to the house early, just to see Jessica. We even found a picture of her in his drawer."

"But she was such a nothing, a fat, insignificant...." Suddenly, Ellen screamed. It looked like she was going to make a run for the belvedere, but Al rounded the table and caught her arm.

"Ellen Humphrey...."

"Whitaker," whispered Meredith.

"Ellen Whitaker, you are under arrest for the murder of your sister, Clara Whitaker."

"She's not my sister," growled Ellen.

"You have the right to remain silent, and anything you say can be held against you in a court of law. You have the right to an attorney." Al turned to Meredith. "Is that it?"

"And if you can't afford one, one will be appointed for you," said Meredith.

Mason sat down. Ellen looked at him. "Call my office," she said. "Tell them I'm sick."

"No," said Mason. "I'm telling the truth."

"I want a lawyer," said Ellen. As Al clipped handcuffs around her wrists, she started to shake.

"That sneaky cow," she muttered.

"Who?" asked Meredith, peering at her. "Clara? Well, she's out of the picture. Now, thanks to you and the Illinois slayer's statute, Alan gets everything."

"He's got his own punishment," said Ellen. "That disgusting old man. With his own daughter-in-law. His son's wife."

"What?" asked Meredith. "Sanford and Jessica?"

"A tiger doesn't change its stripes," said Ellen. Meredith swallowed.

"I get one phone call," said Ellen. "I want to talk to my brother. I have an awful lot to tell him. And Mason," she said, turning to her husband, "I need you to call two lawyers. Call a defense lawyer for me and send him to the Kenilworth police station. And get hold of Marvin Phelps, our trusts and estates lawyer. Ask him whether unborn children inherit when their father dies intestate."

"I believe posthumous children do inherit," said Meredith, as she opened the front door. "Ellen, I'll sit next to you in the car. Al, you'd better put on the child locks. And it sounds like somebody better talk to Alan and Jessica Whitaker again."

Chapter Eighteen

Honking her horn, Meredith zipped her Honda around a hesitant Lincoln Town Car into a parking space at Baker's Square next to Alex's Mercedes. Normally, she was a cautious and polite driver, but in this lot she had to act fast – drivers here routinely underestimated their car size and sometimes confused the brake and the gas pedals. Alex and Meredith both stepped into the June sunshine.

"I'm happy you agreed to see me," said Alex. He leaned over to kiss her, and she backed up a step. "But why are we here?"

"Well, it's near my office, for one thing."

Meredith walked around her car and opened the passenger door. A white leather gym shoe projected toward the asphalt, followed by a leg in compression stockings, capped by a small, neat woman with a gray bouffant. "It's Wednesday -- free pie day," Sara explained to Alex, as she skittered for the front door in time to edge out a lopsided gentleman with a four-pronged cane. "You'd better hurry."

"I didn't know she was coming," Alex murmured.

"Sorry," said Meredith. "She took a cab from her hair appointment to the courthouse, and after all that, I couldn't say no. I swear she has a sixth sense."

They caught up with Sara near the hostess stand, where she casually examined the pie case while nudging ahead of a sixtyish woman and her grandson. "Come here, Meredith." Sara grabbed her daughter's arm and pulled her forward. "The apple is delicious. It has a lot of fruit in it." While the grandmother reached for a dropped juice box, Sara followed the hostess to a table in the middle of the restaurant. "Do you have a booth?" she asked. "We would like a booth." Sara turned her head. "They always try to stick you with a bad table at first," she whispered. "You have to stand up for yourself."

Sara scooted into her bench seat, and Meredith slid in across from her. Alex settled next to Meredith, his leg hugging hers. She moved away a few inches and gave him a look. "Nice to see you, Sara," Alex said. "You're looking well."

"Thank you. What are you going to have?" Sara buried her head in the laminated menu and began reading intently.

"Can we talk?" Alex asked Meredith.

"Mom?" said Meredith. Sara continued to study the salad options. "I don't think she can hear us. What are you going to have?"

"I don't care," Alex said. "The hamburger. I wanted you to know, I did it, I did what you wanted. I moved back in with Shawna and Lex. I walked him last night so that she could get more sleep, and I got up with him once too."

"What a hero. That's more than you did with our kids."

220

"You weren't insane," said Alex. "At this rate, Shawna should be in tip-top condition in a week or so. Then I'll go back to the condo, and we can move on with our lives."

"Alex." said Meredith. "Your eagerness to bale on Shawna is duly noted, but it's going to take a lot longer than a couple of weeks. Babies usually don't sleep through the night for, I don't know, at least three months."

"So I'm supposed to stay with her for the next three months?"

"In the guest room," said Meredith. "Just to be clear."

"Something is making me want a hamburger, I just suddenly have a taste for one," said Sara. What are you going to have, Meredith?"

"I don't know, I have to look at the menu."

A young woman in a uniform that looked like it came from the sexy French maid department of the Halloween Store and a name tag that said Tiffany, stopped at the end of their table and pulled out a pad and a pen. "What would you like to drink?" Tiffany asked.

"You go first," Sara said. "I'm still thinking."

"I think we can order," said Meredith. "I'll have the spinach omelet with unbuttered whole wheat toast and a cup of coffee."

"What kind of pie?" asked Tiffany.

"I don't really want pie," Meredith said.

"You have to have the pie," said Sara. "It's free."

"I'll have the hamburger," said Alex. "And we'll have two pieces of French silk pie to go." He

221

turned to Meredith. "You can bring them home for the girls."

"Aren't you going to eat your pie? I feel funny eating pie alone," said Sara.

"The French silk costs a dollar extra," said Tiffany.

"The apple is very good," said Sara. "You should try it, Meredith. Those kids eat too much sugar."

"I don't want any pie," said Meredith.

"Why are you here if you don't like pie?" asked Tiffany. "It's our specialty."

"Of course I like pie," said Meredith. "Can't you see, I'm trying to be good!"

Meredith turned red. Sara looked at Tiffany. "I'll have a grilled cheese sandwich and a piece of apple pie to go. We'll all have our pie to go." She turned to Meredith. "You're right, we'll eat it later," she said. "Excuse me for a moment. I'm going to the ladies' room."

As Sara inched toward the hostess stand to ask directions to the restroom, Alex took Meredith's hand. She let it rest in his like a limp fish. "I think we're the only people in here between the ages of six and eighty," he said. "It's very romantic." He smiled at her.

She rested her head on his shoulder, just for a moment, and started to laugh. "I knew you'd like it as soon as Mom suggested it," she said. "Sorry about that."

"No, this is fine," Alex said. "It's perfect. We're a family, right? And your mom will be going back to Florida soon. We'll have plenty of time to be alone. The rest of our lives – after this three months of purgatory, anyway."

Meredith traced a blackberry stain in the table top with her finger. "Do you think you're going to make it? I mean, Shawna will start to lose weight, get back in shape. Apparently, based on the fact that you left me for her, she is a very enticing young woman. Blonde. Straight hair. Thirty. And, as you have pointed out to me on numerous occasions since you impregnated her, you are married."

"Meredith." He gripped her hand. "I have learned. I know what I want. I want you. And I want our family."

"All forty-three years and extra ten pounds of me? And Lex is your family too," said Meredith.

"You argue too much," said Alex. "Did anyone ever tell you that you should be a lawyer?" He reached over and touched her cheek. "I love you. I will make this work. I will not neglect Lex, or Maggie, or Lucy. We will make this work."

Sara eased herself back into the booth just as Tiffany appeared with the food. "That was so fast," Sara said to Tiffany. "I don't know how you do it."

"That's okay," said Alex. "Don't tell us. Some things are better kept secret."

"So," said Sara, "I'm glad you were both able to join me for lunch. This is my treat."

"Don't be silly, Mom," said Meredith.

"You are my guests," said Alex.

"No, it's my party and my treat," said Sara. "I wanted to talk to you both about the future." She swiveled to search behind her. "Where is that waitress? I forgot to order a drink." Meredith nibbled an edge of dry toast. "Anyway, I've learned a few things since I've been visiting."

"There's no place like home?" suggested Alex.

"Close," said Sara. "I love being around you, Meredith, and spending time with my granddaughters. I think they like it too, and I know they have benefited. And you're so busy, Dear."

"Of course we all love seeing you too, Mom," said Meredith.

"Yes, well. I do have some very nice friends at Independence Valley, but it's awfully cold in the air conditioning this time of year. It's like living in an ice box!"

"You're welcome to stay longer, Mom," said Meredith. "Here, drink my coffee while you're waiting, I haven't touched it. Do you want any ketchup?"

"Thank you, Dear. Where is that waitress? Alex, could you go find her?" Alex stayed put. "Well, I don't want to impose on you, Meredith. It's too much company already. But," she tapped her hair helmet, "I think I have arrived at the perfect solution." Sara turned to Alex. "So, I understand that you may be moving out of your condo for the next three months."

Alex turned to Meredith. "How did she know that? Wasn't she in the bathroom?"

"Well, if it's just going to be sitting vacant," Sara continued, "I don't much care for your furniture, but the wallpaper is very tasteful, and I love the location. I can walk to the Jewel, and I met a very nice taxi driver. He gave me his card, and he said that I could call him any time. He is from Pakistan. He's very interesting."

"When did you see my condo?" asked Alex.

"Never mind that," said Sara. "I was just thinking, maybe I could house sit for you, while you're living in Kenilworth. I could keep the place straight, make sure pipes don't burst, that sort of thing. And then, in the fall, I could go back to Orlando. I think it would work out perfectly."

Meredith and Alex looked at each other. "I think that sounds like a great idea, Mom," Alex said.

"I'm not your mom," said Sara. "But you are the father of my grandchildren."

"Families are complicated," said Meredith.

"Yes, if you let them be, which, apparently you do. I think I would like to be around for a while, just to keep an eye on things. That condo is half way between your houses. I can keep an eye on both of you."

"That's great, Mom," said Meredith. "I feel like I'm sixteen."

"Then it's settled," said Sara. "I'll call my friend Cora to send me some clothes. I'm sure she won't mind. I gave her that coffeemaker you sent me last Chanukah, with the grinder and the timer. It was very generous of you, Dear, but I never could figure out how to use the thing."

Tiffany stopped by the table. "I'll get your pie now," she said.

Meredith pushed her omelet plate to the side. "And some hot water for my mother, and some more coffee. Also, forget the boxes. We'll eat the pie now. Apple for everyone."

"Oh, goody," said Sara. "Sometimes you just have to let go and enjoy yourself."

Meredith looked at Alex and her mother. She loved them both, and they both drove her crazy. That's what families did. And if she survived the next three months, it would be a bloody miracle.

Shawna bumped the baby carriage out the front door. The sun was shining, and, despite the high body count in this portion of the block, the air smelled clean and promising. Yanking a remnant of yellow police tape from the branches of a blooming pompom bush, she continued down the walk and then stopped on the sidewalk to examine her yard. Dead leaves from last fall had lodged around the bushes and up against the evergreens beside the front door. Now that Alex had moved home, she would ask him to call the yard man to rake, and also to plant some of the little pink and white flowers that everyone around here liked. Shawna wanted to fit in, and Clara's murder in her family room could go either way. If she and Alex neglected their house, she would be the witch in the scary mansion of doom. But, if they mowed the lawn and bought a tasteful welcome wreath for the front door, she might become the intriguing new mom with a tale to tell. Shawna was married to a doctor, she had a baby son, and if she got her hair highlighted and went to church, before long she would be an upstanding member of the community, just like Cece had been.

In other good news, Alex had moved back in. True, he was sleeping on the couch, but that was a start. Between nursing Lex and her new diet regimen, soon she would fit into pants that zip, and then Alex would be back in her bed. He obviously couldn't resist her. She didn't know why she had worried so much about Meredith, who blew every chance she got.

As Shawna passed the spiky wrought iron fence that surrounded the park, she heard the faint tinkling of her cell phone ringing at the bottom of Lex's diaper bag. Reaching into the basket under the carriage, she groped through Pampers and wipes for the vibrating chunk of plastic. It must be Alex, checking on her. She flipped the phone open.

"Hello, Shawna? Shawna Bennett?" An uncertain, but deeply male voice rushed towards her across space and time. "This is Tim, Tim O'Rourke. I don't know if you remember me. We met at Mickey's Saloon, on Pleasure Island in Downtown Disney? I know it's been a while. How are you doing, anyway?"

At first Shawna had thought that moving to Orlando would be fun, bikinis and sun and margueritas far away from Meredith, who was stuck to the bottom of Alex's shoe like a flavorless glob of chewed gum. But it soon became apparent that, despite his admiration for her strategically bronzed and snow white body parts, Alex intended to spend the bulk of his time in the hospital studying decrepit intestines. At least that's what he said. She had given him every inducement she could think of – shiny bra-and-thong sets, candlelit French take-out – she had even baked a goddamn lemon meringue pie from the lemon tree next to their lanai. By September she was so fiercely lonely and furious that she decided to check out a more appreciative environment. She had only wanted a little admiration – at least she thought she did – and what could possibly go wrong in

227

Downtown Disney? How was she to know that grown men attended conventions at Disney hotels, and that a free barge ran on a regular basis between Pleasure Island and the French Quarter Resort? And Tim was over-heated and attentive, and then he was drunk, and so was she, and then – oh, damn it! She had immediately decided to forget the whole thing. She had forgotten it.

"No, I don't remember you. I think you have the wrong number."

"Well, that's too bad. Because I had a great time with you – you are smokin' hot, if you don't mind my saying so. As fate would have it, I'm in Orlando again -- and I was thinking that you and I could get together again, have some fun."

"Well, I'm not in Orlando anymore, and I don't remember you, and I think you should lose this phone number. Enjoy your convention. Goodbye."

Shawna hung up and buried the phone back in the diaper bag. She began to walk briskly, and then to run. Tim meant nothing, he was nothing. She had made it up with Alex the next night, and the night after that too, just to be safe. There was no sense upsetting him, then or now, over ancient history, a mistake she had made and immediately regretted. And now she and Alex had an unbreakable bond. They had Lex. She would never tell Alex that she had doubted him, not ever.

Shawna paused between the two stone churches on Kenilworth Avenue, the fake country English church that Cece had attended, and the castle on the right. She didn't know much about religion, besides Santa Claus and the Easter Bunny, but these places mattered to a lot of people in this community.

If she and Alex started to come here, if Lex were baptized and she sold cupcakes at a bake sale, that would be a fresh start for their family. What had she done, after all? It was just a little slip. Lex looked just like Alex, at least he did in a certain light. He was a baby, he looked like a baby. And he was innocent, and she was just – ignorant. And her motives were good, she was protecting her husband and her child, she was preserving her family. The more she thought about it, the more she realized that she had nothing to be sorry for. Lex started to wiggle, and his eyes popped open, big leering eyes that looked just like Alex's. Shawna turned the carriage around and hurried back home. She and Alex and their son were going to be happy here. Everything was going to be fine.

About the Author

Hope Sheffield grew up in Rochester, New York, and then moved to Memphis, Tennessee, where she graduated from high school. She earned a degree in psychology at Harvard College. Although she greatly enjoyed Harvard Law School, her legal career was brief. She and her husband have four adult daughters and a teenage son. The author now lives with her husband on Chicago's North Shore. *The Poisonous Tree* is her fifth Meredith Bennett mystery, following *Blood Mother*, *The Inflatable Man*, *Turnabout*, and *The Glass Table*.